MR. LEVINS AND ME

Lior Aharon

Mr. Levins and Me

Lior Aharon

Paperback ISBN: 978-1-7382114-0-1

eBook ISBN: 978-1-7382114-1-8

For Shir,

Thank you for reading all my high school essays. I'll bet you thought reading my work would stop there. Here's my novella.

PROLOGUE

MARCH 1968

New York City is truly as exhilarating as everyone deems it to be. I know how repetitive it must be to hear as such. The fantastical promise of the 'Big Apple,' where dreams come true. You may have gotten "New York City is the heart of the United States! The city shows all the glories of being American. Any one person who claims they belong to this land needs to visit." In my youth, I received gasps of disbelief upon revealing that I had never visited the Big City. Always followed by, "Oh, you must—I would live there if it weren't for the kids!"

I am not from New York City. I am not even from New York State. I know what it is like to roll your eyes as everyone suddenly returns from the city with an epiphany. However, allow me to share a secret with you, one that many people have a hard time accepting: when everyone says something is amazing, it probably is. I say "probably" so that you do not condemn me if you happen to disagree. To each their own.

Though, if you are a part of the unfortunate population to have never visited, allow me the honor of enlightening you that it is not just the tourist attractions that enamor those who visit. They are still magnificent, of course. The height that the Empire State Building stands at, the architecture of the Metropolitan Museum of Art, and the emblematic Statue of Liberty—monumental.

However, the people who come here to see a French green sculpture tend to find themselves more impressed by New York City's liveliness. I will not be the first or last to tell you that the citizens shape the city. Currently, to add to the flamboyancy, those in Manhattan are always dressed in the most colorful clothing. Everyone wants to look like Twiggy or Mick Jagger. In the years I have been here, my wardrobe has adopted greens, blues, oranges, and yellows with the luminosity of the hair on troll dolls. It is quite fun.

Buildings surround the perimeter of every edge of the road. Manhattan is the only place where the sky is obstructed at every angle you look at. And when you are not looking at towering buildings, you are looking at lights. These lights are accentuated in the Deuce. Time Square has beautiful theaters, bars, billboards, and neon lights that can brighten even the most melancholic of souls. The simplicity of collective laughter and conversation contributes to the contagious liveliness. After all, Manhattan is nothing without Man.

Broadway allows couples to see musicals live, including ones like the wonderful *West Side Story*. It is the average person's glimpse into the flash and fame of acting. That said, if you are only in New York for the actors, you would be better fit for Los Angeles.

Boldly colored vehicles match the color one feels within the city. If you want to explore other cultures, there are two sectors in Manhattan wholly dedicated to the Chinese and the Italians. Although, if you ask me, Brooklyn is essentially a third sector for the Jews. All excellent places for food.

If you're feeling tired of being impressed by the city and are in search of a reason to complain, then Wall Street is the place for you. Pretentious businessmen gather to discuss investments, stocks, and the economy while battling for virility. A valuable lesson I have learned for all women visiting Manhattan is to avoid the Financial District altogether. Nothing good comes from the Financial District. If you are a woman who accidentally wound up at Wall Street and would consequently like to leave the city entirely, I understand. You can take a taxi to Queens which houses one of the most well-known airports in the United States of America, John F. Kennedy International Airport.

I moved from Hartford, Connecticut several years ago to be a model. My grandparents immigrated to Connecticut from Alcamo, Italy, but I have always been more immersed in New English than Italian culture. Still, there is not much to say about Connecticut apart from the fact that I grew up eating so much seafood that I would get sick.

I never went fishing, but the young boys at school would often tell tales about the fish they caught. The bigger the fish, the cooler you were. Once, a boy made the mistake of telling a girl he was keen on the story of the preparation to catch the fish, rather than the adventurous tales of actually catching it. I watched as the girl looked at him with a disinterested expression until he started to describe how to breed maggots for bait. She shrieked in disgust then ran to tell her girl friends about the freak who breeds maggots. He was alienated for the rest of the school year.

During school, I was predominantly isolated by choice. I had many responsibilities at home and believed that meant I was more mature than every girl in my grade. It's true, I was, but I took it too seriously. I was unfriendly to the girls at school because I thought they were superficial. Again, many were, but as an eleven-year-old, it is fine to have friends that are only there so you have someone to play dolls with.

As I entered the early stages of adolescence, these girls began to resent me, anyway. I was pretty and boys liked me. I almost always dismissed the boys, though. I had not cared much for their attention. This was irregular for a girl my age. I was expected to swoon at the handsome young lads whose gazes frequently rested much below my eyes. I thought they were all foolish. Too immature, too childish. I wish I could say this thought persisted as I grew older. The longing for love and lust catches us all eventually.

At the time, I rejected the young boys gently. Several times, I would say, "I am not yet ready for marriage, certainly another girl is." I might have even supplied them with a name. Really, those girls should have thanked me.

The lecherous glances from men and envious stares from women increased significantly by the time I was fourteen. By then, I realized that if people were always staring at me, I might as well make a living out of it. What better place to do so than the city with a reputation of fulfilling dreams?

Moving here was the best decision I have ever made. New York City is ethereal, and I will never say otherwise, no matter how insufferable you may think me to be for doing so. However, any city, no matter how glamorous, can be hard to appreciate when the love of your life cannot even bring himself to look at you anymore.

MEMORY

APRIL 1965

I am sitting at the Chock Full o' Nuts on 34th street with a cigarette in one hand and a novel in the other. My presence at a coffee shop is not a frequent occurrence. I have only recently started drinking coffee. As a teenager, I never understood where people found enjoyment in a cup of coffee. I thought it was more neat than anything—if you drink a cup of this bitter, gritty, black liquid, your fatigue will disappear! Caffeine is a marvelous thing, coffee is not. Even now, I am only going to order it to stimulate my brain for the morning, though other people seem to love the stuff. Chock Full o' Nuts is always as busy as a bee. This morning, I made an effort to come early to avoid the crowds. Still, there are people, though a tolerable amount. Enough to make the place feel lively without being claustrophobic.

I am sitting at a brown circular table for one. I dressed in a yellow turtleneck with dark blue slim fitting jeans and styled my black hair in a flipped bob this morning.

I cross my legs as I flip my page of Hamlet. I have heard varying criticisms about Hamlet which is what compelled me to read it. I read Romeo and Juliet in the ninth grade and never saw it as anything more than mediocre. I understand the star-crossed lovers concept but I believe it was sold short. Dying as a result of young pruriency and infatuation just did not suffice for me. In fact, I think that their chemistry was void of meaning. How could one love someone without knowing them? They would only be in love with what they have made their lover to be, in love with their own fantasy, their own self.

I believe Hamlet to be different. Hamlet is not only guided by love—whether it is the sexual love for his mother or the familial love for his father is something to be discussed with Sigmund Freud, not me—but also betrayal. I know that people will deem me superficial for declaring Hamlet a victim but I stand firm to it. I understand the intricacies of the play and how Hamlet was selfish, but he was a victim, nonetheless. The only problem is that everyone else is, too. You cannot deem a single character good or evil without ignoring parts of their tortuousness.

Hamlet believes Gertrude to be promiscuous after she quickly remarries to fill the void of her passed husband. Now, she may well be promiscuous, *but* she also may have remarried because she believed that she was worthless unless wed. Only the blissfully ignorant cannot see the gray in a world of black and white.

A waiter approaches me as I take a drag of my cigarette. I can see that he is rushing to get between customers, his stride is slightly paced, though his demeanor does not show it. He stands tall and confident, the posture of a gentleman. He is handsome, too. He has golden blonde hair and deep-set dark blue eyes with low, straight eyebrows. His nose is wide but straight, his lips full but round. He has a figure that is lean though not skinny, providing him with sharp cheekbones and defined muscle. He doesn't look much older than I.

"Hello, ma'am, what can I get you?" he asks. He has a deep, genteel voice with a light New York accent. I wonder if servers are trained to talk in such ways, to allure the customer.

I reluctantly prepare myself to request a coffee but before I get the chance to answer his question, he looks at the play laid upon the table.

"Wow, Hamlet? That's a good one—complex. I studied it during high school. Impressive to read for leisure, ma'am," he says, unaware of his condescension.

"Sir, are you already trying to flatter your way to a generous tip? I haven't even ordered yet," I joke politely.

"Forgive me, it is just nice to see a woman read for once. A beautiful one at that," he says with a wink.

"What a charmer you are," I say sarcastically, cautious of not crossing the line between cordial and scornful. Two sentences into conversation and he has already disappointed me. I do not know when men began to believe that women lost their capability for intellect. It was probably when they began making household chores a defining female characteristic. A man somewhere thought to himself, *How can I take advantage of the people around me even more?* Then decided to revoke women's rights to think. Assigning submissiveness and domesticity to femininity is a clever trap. A woman must only understand manners, cleaning products, and where she lies on the hierarchy of human. A relief from all the cruel realities of life. How simple and breezy. Thank you, men!

"It's a natural-born talent." He smirks at me. I can see that flirting with women is not a foreign affair for him. He continues, "But I sincerely do applaud you. I hope you are enjoying the play."

"You speak as if you wrote it yourself," I reply.

"I could only wish to be so talented."

"Do you write?" I ask.

"No, I'm a photographer. A struggling one, at that, but I'm passionate. I have been since I was a boy," he says, standing up a little straighter.

"What do you photograph?"

"People—but not portraits. I like to capture those who are unaware of it, people are most human when they are oblivious. There is no thought about their pose, no conscience, only their own personality."

He's staring. I hold his eye contact until he notices and gets flustered, looking away.

"What about you?" he asks, seemingly attempting to cover it up. "What do you do?"

"I'm a freelance model."

He frowns, understanding that he just threw an opportunity away before it was even presented to him.

I smile. "A shame about that 'no portraits' thing," I say.

"Maybe I could change," he challenges. But I'm not impressed.

"Maybe," I say dismissively.

He senses that I'm tense. I can see it in his hesitancy.

"I didn't mean to offend," he says. "With the comment about you reading."

"Whatever do you mean?" I ask, feigning a puzzled expression.

"It's not the first impression I wanted to make. You're beautiful, truly, and I can tell that you are an intelligent *person*. I should not have made such a comment."

My puzzlement is genuine now. Most people don't try to fix their bad first impressions. They show who they are and everyone else can either accept it or reject it. Most people do not think to apologize if they make mistakes in their introductions. I can appreciate a person who will admit when they are wrong.

"Thank you for saying that," I say, courteously this time.

"Of course, I would be honored to be able to shoot you one day."

"Excuse me?" This man knows how to take a woman by surprise.

"With my camera! Forgive me, this is really not going in my favor."

I laugh. "I think you're doing all right."

He relaxes at the sound of my laughter and smiles at me. He has dimples that compliment his youthful features.

I inhale a breath. "Though, I'm surprised. I assumed with practice this kind of thing becomes instinctual."

He furrows his eyebrows in confusion. "What kind of thing?"

"The flirting. It's part of the act, no? It comes with the list of skills for the job?"

He smiles as he shakes his head. "Ma'am, you have me mistaken. I may be skilled, but I am not practiced."

I lean toward him slightly. "Why do I not believe you? How can you perfect something you have never tried?"

I see him slightly raise his eyebrow at my implication that he has perfected flirting. "Well, a man who makes himself coffee every day is not a barista, but it does not mean he cannot make himself a good cup of joe," he says with pride, not realizing what he has just admitted. To a woman. A woman he is clearly interested in.

"So, you practice...on yourself? You have become 'skilled' at flirting by practicing on yourself in front of a mirror?"

His face flushes red. "No. No, that is not what I mean. Listen, it is not something you can do without... I don't want to talk about it."

I laugh and roll my eyes. He's likable.

He takes my laughter as an opportunity. "You know, I could start practicing for real. If you're not busy tonight, maybe—"

"James!"

James quickly turns around. "Yes, sir?"

"Is her order long as hell or are you just not taking it?" The man behind the counter yells. He is dark-skinned, fat but short, and nearly balding. However, he seems like the type of man that, when you aren't misperforming on your job, has the biggest heart. That is to say, I have already spoken to him before and he is indeed a sweetheart.

"I'm sorry, Earl. I'll get right on it."

He turns back to me and whispers apologetically, "The old man can be a bummer sometimes."

I think about forgiving and simply forgetting about him, but I decide to play a game instead.

I look at him with a faux-disapproving expression. "Well, *James*, are you going to take my order or not?"

James looks at me wide-eyed for a moment before slyly grinning in understanding. "Of course, ma'am. What can I get 'ya?" he asks in an exaggerated server-voice.

"Just a coffee will suffice."

He bows as if he is serving the Queen of England.

"My pleasure. I'll be back in a moment, Madame."

"Don't let your reflection's charm distract you in there."

"You ask too much of me," he says as he begins walking away.

Several minutes later, he returns with the coffee and a note written on a napkin in pen. I can just make out what it says: "Want to go out on a date with me?"

Very straightforward. I suppose he didn't have room to write much else. He watches me as I read the note. He puts his thumbs up in question. I nod and he smiles wide. He takes my hand, gently kissing it, and continues on to the next customer before his boss takes notice.

The next twenty minutes consist of exchanged glances and sly smiles. When I finish my coffee, I leave him a generous tip as well as a napkin with my name and the words: "Here, next Friday, six o'clock in the evening. I want to hear your thoughts on Hamlet, come prepared."

CURRENT

MARCH 1968

"James…" James Levins is standing inside of my bedroom. His dark eyes quickly move side to side as they look at both of mine. It is such a helpless thing, seeing the hope drain from the eyes of the person you love the most, knowing it was you who caused it. Well, mostly you. He stares at me as if begging for me to deny what he is thinking. To tell him this is a massive misunderstanding. I do not say anything.

I want to run my hands through his hair, I want to tell him that everything will be okay, that we will fix this, but I am not so foolish. Touching him right now would be like touching a rabid dog. Sometimes it's important to keep distance.

Don't get me wrong, it crushes me to see him like this. James has a soul more beautiful than anyone I've ever known. If you told me in April of 1965 that the waiter from the coffee shop would be the man that I end up loving most in this world, I don't think I would have believed you. I knew what men could be. I knew to restrain myself. A naive thought. Love does not listen to your boundaries.

Any woman would have been privileged to be loved by James Levins. There is no person on the planet that could have made me feel so desired, so cherished, so protected. Even when he was angry, he was calm. He never raised his voice. Our arguments felt more like discussions. If I yelled, he listened and replied placatingly. After the fight, I would apologize for yelling and he would reassure me. Sometimes, he just gave in to my side of the argument. Other times, he ensured we compromised, no matter how stubborn I was being. And that was it. He always understood what to do. Nobody has ever understood me like that before. No one ever will again. It felt like there was just not a bone in his body capable of feeling hatred. I suppose that after everything, I am about to discover what it is like to be despised by James Levins.

I look over at the clock and see that fifteen minutes have passed. Neither James nor I have moved. Nothing will ever be the same.

MEMORY

JUNE 1965

We are in James's apartment. We have been on three dates so far, this is the fourth. I have wanted to see him more often, but he has taken up more shifts at work, and I have been getting more modeling gigs.

I still do not know him very well. I know where he's from, that like me, he is an only child, that he recently graduated from Columbia University for Arts and Sculpting since no photography-based programs exist, and that he reads—his favorite book is The Catcher in The Rye by J.D. Salingert. Despite the limited factual information I know about James, talking to him feels as natural as breathing. He is the type of person who makes himself feel familiar to others even if he were a stranger.

James's apartment is not massive, but I have never minded such particularities. With smooth sage walls and a living room large enough to hear the slight echo of Connie Francis' voice as the vinyl record spins, I cannot complain. The apartment has a balcony with a large window leading to it. Rays of sunlight enter through the glass, displaying themselves like jewelry on my skin.

James hovers over his kitchen countertop as he puts film into his camera. I know he wants this to be perfect. Photography is sacred to him. He requested that I wear something I feel best in, so I dressed myself in a strapless black silk dress I recently bought. It is slim enough to emphasize where I curve and where I lay flat but not so revealing as to be deemed provocative. James wears nothing but jeans. Such an artist.

His apartment is decorated with pictures from photographers like a grass field with eggs on Easter. When I asked James which photos are his, he led me only to one, an image right beside the entrance. I asked him why, as a photographer, he would only frame one photo of his. He said that he believes that displaying any others would diminish the influence of this one.

It is of a father and son. There are passersby in the background, but James composed the image to highlight the two specifically. The son is no more than a year old and his father looks to be in his early twenties. The father is carrying his son with one hand, excitedly whispering to him as he points toward something out of frame. James titled it "Boyhood."

"The father's boyhood is reborn through the birth of his son," he explained. "They are both experiencing adolescence together in entirely different stages of their lives."

James also takes the time to tell me all about the Nikon F 33mm camera he will be using. He tells me about its versatility. How its titanium shutter frame can shoot up to four frames per second with two-hundred and fifty different exposures. He tells me about the "revolutionary" instant-return mirror and aperture.

To be frank, I do not care about any of it. I appreciate photography, but I do not understand the technology. The singular reason I would go on to remember all he said—why I am able to recite this information—is because I always want to listen to him speak. I like hearing his thoughts about things, no matter the subject. He could lecture me on the history of the spoon, and I would be attentive for every word.

James has set up the wall to tape extremely large paper to form the background. His furniture is clustered to one side of the room while James stands at the other.

"Okay, it looks like I am just about ready," he says.

I take a deep breath and walk in front of the white screen. I have done this before. Many others have taken my picture. But the way James confidently maneuvers himself, like he has been thinking about doing this since the day we met. Despite both our confident fronts, we are placing ourselves in vulnerable positions. I know that James wouldn't do this for just anyone, and I know that I will let him direct my pose anyway he wants. His vision as a photographer says a lot about him as a person—whether he chooses to take advantage of my willingness to participate the way he pleases. But his directions are never lascivious: move my chin a little to the left, look up at him slightly.

I can tell when he is trying to depict me as powerful and when he is trying to depict me as innocent. After a while, I notice that he has favored the powerful. He allows me to look down at the camera, leaning on furniture like I'm the man.

"You're breathtaking," he says, looking at me from behind the viewfinder. This is the first time he has spoken since we started. I notice that he is silent when he is creative.

"I have grown into my looks."

"I don't believe that. I think men have been toppling over just to get a good look at you your whole life. You could make a man object at his own wedding."

I smile softly. "That's kind of you to say."

"Only the truth."

Another silence.

"What about you?" I ask. "You haven't had women collapsing just to get a look at you?"

He smiles. "A few. Not important ones. I think that the only one I met on the way down was you."

I imagine both of us passing each other on the street, falling in each other's arms because we quickly wanted to get one last lustful glance at the other. Things that only happen on screens in front of audiences.

"Why modeling?" he asks, interrupting my daydream.

"Why photography?" I retort.

He looks at me skeptically. "That's no fun."

"What's no fun?"

"Avoiding my question so blatantly. You hadn't even considered answering it."

"Oh, please. I know that you are sensitive, James, but you could not possibly be hurt by that," I say. He frowns.

Having been in James's presence for a total of twelve hours, I have become comfortable being near him. And I have noticed that he is a very mellow man. Of course, he can be sociable, but he mostly keeps to himself. He does not have many friends—he loves selectively. He does not attempt to be the manliest person in the room. He is content just the way he is.

"I was not hurt by it, only disappointed." He pauses for a moment and then says, disbelievingly, "Also, 'sensitive', really?"

I smile at the irony of his defensiveness. "You only question that because you are not seeing yourself the way I am right now. You are very sensitive. But it's nothing to be ashamed of. In fact, I think it's one of the best things about you."

"The fact that I'm a little bit girly?"

"The fact that you have a soul."

A pause. Then, "Why do you model?"

I sigh and give him an answer that I think will satisfy him. "I like to be the person that represents other people's ideas. I like to be a symbol."

This is not completely untrue. I do like the concept of representing something larger. But if I cared that much about such things, I would have become a physicist. I am primarily a model for money. But I know that James is not a photographer for that reason, and I know he would not let me hear his if I did not say my own. However fabricated it may be.

"Now, it's your turn. Why street photography?"

He takes a few steps back to get a full body shot, curving his back to align the lens with my torso. "I love people," he says. "I love that no person is not one single thing and how statistically, that means the exact same person will never exist. I get to look at them and try to guess which of those traits they acquire and what that makes of them."

Unlike myself, James believes it is possible that good can outweigh bad and vice versa. He told me about this on our first date when I asked about his opinions on Hamlet over coffee. Or rather, I did not ask, he had handwritten a four-page-long essay regarding his thoughts on the characters, plots, and themes.

Many men would have been immediately repelled by the offer I proposed. A date where a man does not talk about himself is preposterous. James accepted it readily. In fact, his greeting to me, before "Hello," was, "I don't think I was able to write everything. I reread the play and revised my work from high school, but I can definitely discuss beyond what I've written. How would you like to start?"

We sat at that coffee shop and talked until closing.
He spoke about how the female characters were used as
a pawn for the men's schemes, how Hamlet was
egotistical, how Horatio symbolized the light in the
darkness and how his life is forever tainted by Hamlet's
treatment of him. I shared my belief about goods and
evils, he disagreed, and we argued.

"How could you say that he was justified?" he said.
I sighed. "I'm not saying he was justified but I'm sure
Hamlet did not ever plan to be a murderer in his life.
How could he have known any better with what he
was given?" And as I listened to him explain himself, I
realized how willing I was to see his point and how he
was with mine. I wanted to continue to ask him
questions, and I wanted to hear his answers, even if I
disagreed with them. When we had to part, James
asked if he could see me again, to which I replied, "Was
that not a given?"

James adjusts the lens on his camera.

"You can see all that based on a fleeting moment?" I
ask him. "One photograph determines a person's
character?"

"I cannot say that my 'evaluations' are always
accurate, but everyone has their idiosyncrasies that
even they don't know about."

How curious. "What's mine?"

He barely takes a moment to think about it before
he swiftly but drastically switches positions. His
movements are purposeful. He takes a few steps
forward and kneels down in front of me. The focal is

now directed at my hands. I can see the lens expand and then close as the shutter captures the image.

"That. You run your thumb over the beds of your nails often." My fidgeting fingers slow to a stop.

"You did it when I first approached you, you did it on our first date while I uncontrollably talked about Hamlet, you did it when I told you about my family on our last date, and you're doing it now. I can't tell what the trigger for it is. Boredom, intrigue, nervousness..."

"Well, I was never bored so you can remove that from the list."

He looks up from the viewfinder now. "And so there were two. Which one is it?"

"It's a habit that I am not even aware of myself, remember? I couldn't tell you if I wanted to."

He shrugs nonchalantly. "I'll figure it out eventually."

"I wouldn't be so sure."

"What makes you say that?"

"Intrigue and nervousness can be interchangeable."

He arches an eyebrow. "Sure, for some, but something tells me that the two look different for you."

"What do you mean?"

He shrugs. "I don't think people make you nervous. I believe that you think people don't know you. What's there to be nervous about if no one knows anything about you? To be a model but to not feel seen. Sounds Shakespearean in itself."

"You're observant."

He holds up the camera. "I have to be—my paycheck depends on it."

I laugh.

"Most people would be angry at me for saying all that, you know? I don't think being analyzed is a very serenading thing to a woman."

"Oh, it's all right. I'm not bothered."

"Why not?"

"Would you like me to be?"

He laughs a little. "No. It's just curious, is all."

"Well, if people can't make me nervous, why should they make me uncomfortable?"

"Ah," he says.

Then he looks at me earnestly. "You know, if you let me, I'd like to be the first person to be exempt from that. I rather have to apologize for making you uncomfortable than knowing nothing I say impacts you at all. I don't want to just be another blurred face in a crowd of those who don't know you."

"You won't be," I say. James smiles softly in response. I look back at the camera and he takes another picture.

MEMORY

JANUARY 1966

"Happy birthday to you…" James looks at the cake that rests in front of him with a flushed face. I tried my best. It is a chocolate cake with a generous amount of vanilla frosting slathered in swirls all around it. I had put the cake in the refrigerator before applying the frosting to prevent any crumbs from flying into the whites of the cake. If you ever attempt to make a chocolate cake with white frosting, put it in the freezer. The fridge does not work.

Atop the cake, swirls of icing align the inner circumference, framing the pink candles that surround the cake. In a nearly illegible font, pink icing reads: "Happy Birthday James!" When I brought the cake out, James burst into fits of laughter.

I frowned at him, insisting that it was the best I could do, and he said, "I know it is, darling. I'm sorry. This is the best thing I could have asked for."

I rolled my eyes. "Don't get all sentimental on me," I said. He laughed. "Believe me, if I'm crying, it will not be because I'm sad."

As I sing to him, James is actively withholding his giggles. I am so happy about it.

Initially, James and I planned on going to James's mother's house for his birthday. His mother, Elizabeth, does not have a driver's license of her own, so anytime one wants to see the other, James drives to Brooklyn. They celebrated together for every birthday of his life. This year, plans were changed.

Last night, there was a terrible blizzard. Two feet of snow rest on New York like a blanket finally tucking the city in to sleep. It was perfect. I am not ready to meet his mother, and I hadn't prepared an excuse as to why I couldn't accompany him yet. James was disappointed that he couldn't spend this time with his mother, so I made sure that he would still have a birthday he could enjoy, just the two of us.

I have never had a proper birthday, not like James has. My mom used to give me fifty cents and tell me to buy something from the market. I would either have come home with codfish, or I would have gone to a movie theater by myself. That being said, I do not know how to throw birthday parties. I haven't bothered to celebrate my birthday as an adult. It has never mattered to me. But it matters to James and I wanted to make this feel special for him.

In movies, I have seen people bake cakes, blow out candles, wear party hats, and decorate rooms with balloons. I did not buy any hats, but in James's apartment, I have blown up and placed many balloons floating from the dining chairs. It's not too shabby.

"...Happy birthday, dear James. Happy birthday to you. Make a wish!"

He closes his eyes, smiling wide, then blows out his candles. I lean down to kiss him.

"What did you wish for?"

"Isn't it forbidden to tell?"

"It is?" I look around. "I don't think anyone will know if you say."

"All right." He comes close to my ear as if he is telling me a secret in a crowded room. "Nice try," he whispers.

I shove him away.

He laughs. "Hey! That's no way to treat a man on his birthday."

"Eat your cake, Mr. Levins."

"'Mr. Levins?' Are you trying to reiterate that I'm aging?" he asks, leaning toward me with a smile.

"Yes, actually. Soon those gray hairs will be making their appearance," I say, feigning a serious expression. But it breaks as soon as he kisses me again.

When our lips separate, I say, "It's rude to leave a cake untouched in front of the person who baked it."

I grab a chunk of the cake and smear it on his mouth.

He stands up and takes a few steps back. He swipes his finger on his chin, collecting the excess frosting and licking it clean.

"The only reason your face is not covered entirely in cake right now is because this is delicious and cannot be wasted," he says.

I walk up to him and kiss off the frosting that remains on his top lip.

"Hm, you're right," I say.

He leans over the table to slather more cake on his lips. "Care for another taste?"

"I would love to play this game, but you still have a present you need to open."

"Aren't you a present enough?"

I smile despite myself, and I go to get his present that I have been hiding in my purse. It is a new camera, a 35mm Minolta SRT 101. I know nothing about it. The man at the store told me that it has a shutter speed of up to one-thousandth of a second. James taught me that the smaller the fraction of a shutter speed, the faster it can capture moving objects. One-thousandth is a small fraction. I reckoned that that was quite impressive and decided to purchase it.

He leans over the table as he opens the box slowly. His eyes widen when he sees the camera. He turns to me.

"I can't accept this."

That is not the reaction I was hoping for.

"Yes, you can, and you will."

"These cameras cost a fortune. I couldn't!"

He's right, it did. Luckily, I had some money set aside to buy this beautiful silver and diamond necklace I have wanted for years. It hugs the neck in silver swirls, with five evenly-spaced small flower-shaped diamonds distributed around the piece. I had been putting aside money after every paycheck I have received to one day purchase it. My savings had gotten close. I could have afforded it by the autumn season. I would rather James have this, though. The necklace would not bring me the happiness that seeing James use this camera will. And I am not going to allow him to refuse.

"It is yours, my dear. I love you. I want you to enjoy this."

His eyes widen again. The blue in his irises as clear as day. This is the first time either of us has said "I love you" to one another.

His dimples shine bright as he smiles wide. "I love you. I love you immensely. Thank you for doing all this for me, you are unbelievable."

He grabs my face and kisses me. This time, I let him.

MEMORY

AUGUST 1966

It is approximately eight in the morning. James is in the washroom brushing his teeth. I spent the night yesterday—though not in the way you think.

Yesterday, we had dinner, and I drank more wine than my brain could resist. As I began to attune to the euphoria of intoxication, James had already begun preparing a glass of water to sober me up and a made bed for me to sleep in. He slept on the couch. When we awoke, I feared that James would be upset for my inconsiderate and irresponsible actions the night before. Instead, this morning, I was greeted by him shirtless, clothed only in his boxers, and he simply said, "Good morning. I hope you're feeling alright, you were pretty drunk yesterday. You can get ready in the bathroom. Your purse is on the coffee table if you need it. I'll get ready right after you, so take your time. I'll prepare you a shot of vodka to get rid of the hangover and strawberries to get rid of the taste."

I already took the shot, now I am eating the strawberries. I have never liked vodka. Truthfully, I do not know how people can drink anything other than red wine.

"James, would you come here for a moment?"

"In a second!" he calls, mouth full of toothpaste.

James still works at the coffee shop but has fewer shifts. He wants to begin taking photography more seriously. I am not sure how that works. I get jobs when they come by. Maybe photography works differently. All I know about photography is what I've been told from him. Truthfully, before James, the only photographer I knew was Robert Frank and that was mostly because I took delight in his name entirely consisting of first names.

I know that James is an ardent advocate of Gary Winogrand, a fellow Jewish, New Yorker street-photographer. James insists he isn't biased in his liking for him, and I am inclined to believe him solely because he is my boyfriend. James also loves Alfred Eisenstaedet's work. He is obsessed with the photograph of the soldier kissing the nurse in Times Square after the war ended. A talented photographer indeed, but James is truly enamored by those pictures. He will stare at them for hours.

I appreciate many women in the modeling industry—the work Twiggy is currently doing is revolutionary—but I am a dilettante in the field. People pay me to pose in front of a camera, and I go home. It's not a bad career, but I cannot say I love it. I sometimes wish I had what James does. His passion, his optimism, his authenticity. But I do not want to envy, so I try to love him for it.

James comes into the room with an unlit cigarette hanging from his lips. He is wearing green plaid trousers and a bright lime green knit t-shirt. He hasn't had the time to gel his hair into a combover so it lies naturally in a graduated side-part. I like it.

He gestures to his outfit. "What do you think? Groovy, right?"

"I really like your hair styled this way."

"What?" he mutters, the cigarette taking up the space his words would escape through.

"I think you should stop applying gel," I say, tilting my head as I look at him.

"So, there is no comment on the outfit."

"You look very fashionable," I say impassively. It is not my favorite.

"You did not even attempt to make that sound sincere," he says with a frown. He takes out a lighter and lights the cigarette.

I walk up to him. "You look incredibly handsome, my dear," I say as I put both hands on his chest. He smiles at me. Then I take the cigarette from his mouth and put it out on a plate.

"Wh—hey!" he protests.

"You don't want those fancy new trousers being sprinkled with ash, do you?" That is partially why I did it. Second being that I don't like to talk to people when they have a cigarette between their lips. It's an inconvenience for all participants of the conversation.

He flattens said trousers with an exasperated sigh. "I've been trying to get into the clothing trends lately. If everyone looks like a traffic light walking down the street, then I might as well join them."

His eyes widen, showing that his previous statement just provoked a fascinating thought. "Do you think that the roads are more dangerous with all these colors?"

I laugh at his absurdity and he continues, "No, really! Picture being a taxi driver. You are making... How much money do they make in an hour? Two bucks? A buck and a half?" I shrug.

"Sure, all right, a buck and a half," he says, gesturing like a businessman, which typically would not be my favorite, but it's James. All his mannerisms are my favorite.

"So you're miserable—driving people while they play bingo in the backseat. Your life sucks. And then you approach an intersection at the Deuce. Now, there's always people at the Deuce, you got to be careful here. So you stop, you're waiting for people to jaywalk and then you realize, 'Goodness gracious, are they jaywalking or is the light red and they're crossing?' So you're looking around trying to spot the traffic light and there is just an endless sea of color! What're you going to do, stop at a green light and get a ticket? Not with a dollar-fifty wage you won't. So, naturally, you keep driving."

This is the most I have ever seen James embrace his Brooklyn identity. It feels like he has bottled up most of it and decided that now is the time for its release. Although James has always had a soft Brooklyn accent, this hypothetical story really accentuates it. He ignores all the 'r's in words and pronounces most of his vowels as 'aw.'

"Immediately, you hit a speedbump. And you're sitting there thinking, 'A speedbump in the middle of the street? What's going on? What's happening?' Then, people are furiously banging on your window and bam! You realize that you just ran someone over."

I gasp. "I know!" he replies fervidly.

"See, honey, you see the dangers of these trends? An old man like me wearing this?"

"Old man? You're twenty-three!"

"Twenty-three with a care for the poor suffering taxi-drivers out there!"

I smile at him. I am going to a photoshoot soon and got ready before James woke up. I am wearing a simple yellow baby doll dress. A headband sits atop my black hair, puffed in the back. I have put on a baby-blue eyeshadow with a small wing of eyeliner, some pink blush, and mascara. I tried to imitate Twiggy's bug-eyed look by applying generous quantities of mascara to my top eyelashes and extra to my bottom eyelashes so they clump together. To accent the shape, I drew miniature triangles on my lower eyelid using liquid eyeliner.

I had to rush my makeup because we woke up late. I was planning on leaving immediately, but I do not want him to go yet.

"Dance with me," I say.

The words escape my mouth before I can think better of it. This was not my intention when I called him over. I wanted to ask him which color lipstick he preferred on me before we left.

"What?" he asks, caught off guard. His surprise is reasonable. My request is abrupt and we need to leave for work. Especially after his bright-colored-clothes-devastating-the-lives-of-taxi-drivers fiasco. Yet that is exactly why I want this time with him. I want to dance with the only man who makes me laugh.

I walk past him to the entrance of his bedroom. There, near the door frame, he keeps his stacks of records from varying musicians: The Beatles, The Mamas & The Papas, The Beach Boys. James is into rock and roll. I think that he was born at a time perfect for his music preferences. Personally, I have never enjoyed rock and roll at all. I can appreciate certain songs by The Beatles, though I favor musicians like Frank Sinatra, Nat King Cole, and Patsy Cline. I love their soothing voices, the way their melodies remind me of being a young girl. I think that I will never be able to appreciate new music like I do theirs.

I look through the stack of records and choose one of Billie Holiday's. "I'll Be Seeing You" begins to play.

"Come." I take James's hand and lead him to the center of the living room.

I place his right hand on my waist and my left on his shoulder. Our other hands hold one another. He looks at me beneath golden eyelashes, his furrowed eyebrows displaying his confusion at this random act of affection. I can see him contemplating whether he should stop me and ask if everything is all right. He doesn't. He relaxes and lets me rest my head on his shoulder. Soon after, he begins to sway with the music. He shifts his hand to my lower back and slowly leads me downwards. He follows down to kiss me very softly. This is not a kiss of passion, this is unadulterated admiration. It makes me melt. The song ends and we do not stop. The only time James moves away is to spin me. He stares as he does so. He is savoring this.

"Where did you learn to dance?" I ask him as he reels me back in.

He takes a deep breath before he speaks, "My father taught me when I was a boy. My mother was not ecstatic about it. She feared that being taught something so intimate by my father would turn me into a homosexual. My father laughed at her for it. Ironically, he wanted to teach me for my future wife. He said that every man needs to know how to lead in a way that makes his woman feel cherished."

"He was a great teacher, I feel very cherished," I say matter-of-factly.

He looks down at me. "That is all I want for you, my love."

CURRENT

MARCH 1968

James abruptly stands. He begins to walk back and forth, not pacing but sauntering, which is somehow more unsettling. James knows how to move his body. I can almost find humor in the fact that in situations like these he still directs himself with grace. Once, he moved genially for me, swaying in time with keys on piano or the strum of guitar strings. Now each step represents a thought. He ponders what words to say, whether I deserve a response at all. After a while, he finally speaks.

"You betrayed me."

That's not fair. That's not fair at all.

"You deceived me."

This was never supposed to happen. This could have been perfect.

"You manipulated me."

Honestly, I am not even sure where this accusation comes from. Or whether these are accusations at all. It feels more like he is revising facts than confronting me.

He stops and turns to face me. "You...How could you?

He does not say it in despair but rather like he genuinely does not understand. The same way you would ask someone to rephrase their explanation to a concept in a math class. I wish he didn't say it at all. Only James would say, "How could you?" instead of, "How dare you?" This perplexes him more than it is infuriating him. I would expect that if he were any other man, I would have been beaten to death by now. But here, James Levins is asking for an explanation, a reason as to why I did this. Something to make sense of the unorthodox predicament he has found himself in. How can I defend myself if he doesn't allow me to be mad at him? Hatred is easy, hatred is comfortable, yet he is giving me no opportunity to hate him back.

I don't know what to do.

<u>MEMORY</u>

JANUARY 1967

"God dammit!" I yelp. Blood begins to puddle on the cutting board. The sliced potatoes look like they have been glazed with ketchup in advance. I tightly wrap gauze around my wound and apply pressure with a squeeze like my mom taught me to do. When the gauze turns entirely red, I replace it with a new one. As soon as the bleeding stops, I discard the potatoes in the trash, sanitize the cutting board, and start anew.

I hate blood. I once met someone who had a crippling fear of seeing blood. Ironically, it was a woman. I was very confused about how she dealt with that every month. But I do not hate blood because it scares me. I only hate the reminder that blood is all I am. Blood and organs in a sack of skin. It makes me feel like an existentialist, something I find no use in being.

I am surprising James by preparing dinner for us both. He said he was going to return from work a little later today and that I did not have to wait at his apartment for him. So, I decided to make his favorite meal of the few that I can prepare. Fish and chips.

I was born and raised in Connecticut. It is no surprise that the only recipes I know predominantly consist of fish. I do make succulent clam chowder though. The key is to be moderate with the cream and add cornstarch if the chowder is still runny. Though, James says that he would rather learn how to cook from scratch than put "such a thing" into his mouth. He has only had clams that have been incorporated into pasta.

James, being from Brooklyn, grew up with matzoh ball soup, kugel, and challah from his family and pizza, spaghetti with meatballs, and calamari from his old Italian friends. There were many Italians in my hometown, too. They always had thick accents and discussed the beauty of their culture. I would listen in awe, not understanding why my household did not sound like theirs did.

My parents were born and raised in Connecticut too, my grandparents were the ones who immigrated from Italy. For my whole life, all the meals I have prepared have been exclusively English. However, James praises Italian cuisine like it's a religion. Fish and chips were the compromise between what I know how to make and what he loves. The New English version of calamari, if you will.

My favorite New English fish are lobster rolls. I've only had it twice before because they cost a fortune, but they are decadent. One day for James's birthday I'll treat him to a lobster dinner. That way, he can comprehend that Connecticut food is not all bad.

Although, to be fair, James does have a remarkable palate. We have gone to some of his favorite places like Russ & Daughters and the 2nd Avenue Delicatessen both on the Lower East Side. I always tell James that one day, I will broaden the variation of what I cook, that I'll buy different cookbooks as a start. Today is not that day.

In two separate bowls, I have prepared the dry ingredients: pastry flour, kosher salt, and baking powder. And the wet ingredients: eggs and water. I dip the fish filets into the wet mixture, then the dry mixture twice. I brace myself as I put the first fish filet in, only relaxing when I hear the ordinary placid sizzle. The oil does not overflow, everything is fine.

I am not unfamiliar with making this dish, this must be my hundredth time doing so, but once, when I was eleven, I didn't batter my filet properly. I am not sure how, but when I placed the fish in the pan, it practically exploded. Hot oil splattered on my arm and on the floor. My mom was furious. After screaming at me for my incompetence, she bent me over and spanked me—which is such a peculiar punishment for a child, but that is besides the point—for both ruining dinner and my arm. I am twenty years old and I still get nervous that the oil will explode.

I was responsible for making dinner most days. My mom never had the time. Her predicament was not an easy one. Both my parents were involved in the war efforts before I was born. My dad was recruited in 1942 and my mom was a voluntary participant in the

Nurse Cadet Corps. She liked the idea of receiving a free education since her own mother spent her years making her living as a hooker. My mom knew she wanted children after the war and preferred to be employed to help with the household finances as much as possible. My parents got married only five months after they met in September of 1941, when they were eighteen and twenty-three. They loved each other, but they also suspected that the USA would begin drafting for the war soon and wanted to avoid it.

They were proven right when the bombing of Pearl Harbour happened in December of that year. However, their attempt at avoiding the war was too late. My dad had already registered for the draft the previous year when he was eligible for mandatory resignation. He was drafted in January of 1943. When he came back, he was alive, but he was not well. My mom was more resilient to what she faced. Though her conditions too were harsh, and she had to make challenging decisions, she felt privileged to have saved so many soldiers' lives.

My parents decided to conceive a child immediately after they came home. I was born nine months later in September of 1946. Apparently, I was supposed to have a twin brother, but I absorbed him in the womb. My mom laughed when she first told me about that, saying that "it fit my personality to do so."

Although the war had ended, it did not leave our household. My dad lost both his legs and his sanity. War neurosis took over. He could not handle the crackling sounds of a sunny-side up egg in the morning or the sound of a kettle. Every Independence Day was a nightmare. While people set fireworks in celebration, my mom would cradle my dad until the noise stopped. This persisted through most of my childhood. My mom would be so worried about my dad that she would forget about me.

PAST

1959

"The End" fades into light on the television screen. I lean toward it to absorb any glimpse I can store into my memory. I want my mind to be my own personal movie theater, built so that I can rewatch that film again and again in my head.

Roman Holiday is just astounding. I have never felt so moved by people on a screen. I typically do not have much time for leisure. Mom does not allow it. There is always something to do around the house before I have the opportunity to sit and watch television. Today, I happened to finish all my chores a little early.

The first of my chores is cooking dinner. Supper for today was a clam linguine. I overheard the recipe from a girl talking to all her friends about it. She's Italian, too. She said that her Ma prepared it for dinner and it had her whole family absolutely elated. My family dinners are always silent. It's not horrible, it is simply what we do. But the idea of my family joyfully eating together, possibly even expressing their gratitude, sounded delightful. I thought that it could be the beginning of us three acting like a real family. Like the ones in the television shows.

As the girl told her friends about the recipe, I retrieved a pencil and paper and copied it all down. I came home, did all my homework (curse all the mathematicians and their theorems), and I began to cook. The Italian girl never mentioned any seasonings so the linguine came out quite bland, but I was proud of it nonetheless.

I sat in the dining room and excitedly waited for Mom and Dad to meet me for dinner. Soon after, Mom came downstairs with Dad. She carried Dad to his chair at the dining table and kissed his temple before sitting down and looking at what rested on her plate. I tried to restrain my hopeful expression. I could not wait for her reaction. She stood up and grabbed the wine bottle that rested in the center of the dining table. *She wants to drink before eating,* I thought. *That isn't anything strange.* Then, with the hand not holding the bottle, she slapped me across the face. I put a hand to my cheek and looked up at her. *Maybe she could tell that I forgot to add seasoning,* I thought. But my punishments were usually spankings. She never touched my face.

Afterwards, Mom simply pushed her chair in and proceeded upstairs. Dad and I continued to sit on opposite ends of the table and eat in silence, just like yesterday.

When we finished eating, I carried Dad to his bedroom. Typically, Mom does this, since I still struggle with it. But I didn't want to wait for her to come downstairs again. I wanted to avoid her for the rest of the day. So, as soon as I heard that she was in the bathroom, I brought Dad upstairs and returned to the living room to complete the rest of my chores.

I washed all the dishes, swept the whole first floor, and dusted and organized the living room. Everything was finished by ten o'clock—that is when I began watching *Roman Holiday*. It is midnight now.

Mom would go absolutely mad if she saw me sitting and watching some romance movie. Luckily, she is distracted putting Dad to sleep. She probably finished most of that bottle she was drinking, so she too should be asleep soon. Sometimes I cherish these moments. When Mom drinks enough, she doesn't bother me and I am left to watch television in the living room. I am happiest when I am immersed in another person's life.

Most of the time, the only thing on is *I Love Lucy* on CBS. I watch it, though I can never really understand what is happening. I just like how dramatic it is. All the whimsical actors and humorous dialogue. But nothing I have ever seen is quite like *Roman Holiday*.

The movie takes place in Rome, Italy. Italy is a beautiful place. I never would have known. I have asked Mom before if we could visit. Maybe if Nana were still alive, she would have wanted to go with us. But Mom forbids it, insisting that we do not have the money or time. It is such a shame. I think I will go anyway when I am older. When I have money of my own and Mom has no control over me, I will leave and I will visit Italy. Just like Audrey Hepburn and Gregory Peck. I'm excited already! Audrey Hepburn's natural glamor makes Italy seem like a dreamland more than it already does on its own. And do not get me started on Gregory Peck. What a dreamboat. A marvelous actor too, just marvelous! And their relationship is most charming. Any girl would feel enchanted watching their relationship blossom. But, in my opinion, that is not all that makes this film as amazing as it is. I especially liked that Joe Bradley and Princess Ann did not love each other instantaneously. That only after she removed herself of her royal facade did he fall in love with her. It was her true self that he loved, not the riches. And I just loved the ending. The tragedy of it. The fact that love does not always have a Happily Ever After. I love that Joe could love Ann without once asking her to stay. He knew that it could not be and he loved her in spite of that.

Could a man really do that for a woman? Love her for nothing more than who she is. Understand her so completely that he does not need words to communicate his hurt having to love and let go. Oh, Joe Bradley.

I imagine myself in Princess Ann's place. A life where everyone is fighting to please you. A life filled with so many luxuries that they no longer amount to anything. Never being satisfied until you are shown what it means to love someone. To live and to love.

I hope that one day, a tall, handsome, and gentlemanly man comes to my house just for me. I hope we spend the night going to parks, theaters, and dances. He will fall for me as I will for him. Then, when we return to my house at dawn, I hope he leans in close to my ear and whispers, "I'll see you next time." A promise that will be ours alone.

I am forced out of my fantasy when I hear Mom close the door to her and Dad's bedroom. She continues walking down the hallway and toward the stairs. She is going to see me watching television late at night. She is going to be furious.

I immediately rush to turn the television off and sit back down on the couch. I straighten my back and stare at the wall. I do not move a muscle. I do not wish to provoke her.

The bottle of wine is still in her hands. Approximately a quarter of it remains. No surprise. She walks up to me and lazily collapses on the opposite end of the couch to me. We sit in silence for a while before she begins to talk.

"You're lucky," she says. Her speech is slurred and her syllables dragged. It almost makes her sound like she is thinking hard about what she is about to say.

"When I was your age…How old are you?"

Clearly, she isn't.

"Twelve," I say.

"Twelve. And cooking linguini, watching television alone at night. Trying to avoid me." She scoffs. "When I was twelve, I would sit and cry waiting for my mom to return home. That was my television. I didn't know how to cook or how to clean—like you do. Oftentimes, Ma would come home past midnight, and I wouldn't eat at all. It's not that she didn't know how to cook. Nonna used to make these meals for her...these special Italian meals. Ma would tell me about it any chance she got. Taunting me. Too busy in alleyways to cook anything herself."

She takes my face in her hands, fingertips digging into my cheeks. "And now look at *you*. Look at what you have. I am at home with you every single day. I've taught you how to cook, how to support your family. You never cry. You're never left waiting. And all of it is because of me. Because I learned it for you."

She lets go of my face, instead using her hand to recklessly swing her wine bottle around. "Yet that's not good enough. You still want these fancy Italian dinners...that I can't teach you. That I can't give to you. Watching television alone while I...Spoiled child. So Goddamn spoiled."

I have no idea what she is talking about. I think she recognizes my confusion because she sighs heavily.

"Christ, you don't get it...Just stick to clam chowder, all right? That's...that's it. Just that." She finishes the wine bottle and returns upstairs. Tomorrow, I will make clam chowder.

1961

"Mom?" I call from downstairs. I place my school bag on the floor beside the entrance to our house.

I am only in my second month of my sophomore year and I am already behind. My teachers don't understand that I have a life beyond a classroom. They are always nagging at me. "Did you finally read the textbook homework from last night?" they often say. My math teacher even gave me notable lecture not so long ago: "It is September and you are already behind the rest of the students in your class. No man wants a stupid girl. If you want a life beyond being a maiden or a whore, you need to start taking responsibility. No excuses, and no flirting with Tony during class. Tony's a bright kid. He doesn't need some sleazy girl distracting him. You focus on your work."

He said that one right before spanking my bottom with a cane three times in front of the class. Mr. Bowers. A rotten old man. His own wife would have been better off being a maiden.

He's also wrong. I don't initiate the flirting with Tony, Tony does! A bunch of the boys do. I never give any of them the time of day anyway. Except for Tony. When Tony offers to help me with my math homework after school, I accept. We don't do anything crazy, it is always in a public library, after all. I did kiss him once, though, between the bookshelves of the history section. It was my first kiss ever.

Kissing is the only thing we have done together (we're not going steady or anything). Kissing was not as magical as I was expecting it to be, but I think that I am just not in love with him yet. You need to be in love to feel the magic.

Boys are the only ones who try to talk to me. Girls at school still do not like me. They didn't last year or the year before that either. I don't mind. I do not have time to try and make friends anymore. If they thought I was a loner when I was twelve, then I will be a loner at fifteen. It does not make any difference to me. People are fools, all of them just fools!

"Mom, are you home?" I repeat.

"Yes," she says from upstairs. "Yes, where else would I be?" She sounds frustrated. Another bad day. I hear her say something to Dad before she rushes downstairs. She looks at me with wide, tired eyes. A knitting needle is shoved through her knotted hair, barely keeping it out of her face. She has deep eyebags that make her look like a skeleton. She didn't sleep last night. Neither did I.

Sometimes, Dad gets these nightmares. Ones that cause him to wake up screaming in the middle of the night. Mom has to hug him tight while he cries himself back to sleep. I used to go to their room when it happened. I would just watch as Mom rubbed his back and rocked him in her arms. Eventually, I would get tired again and return to my room. But she doesn't sleep for the rest of the night when it happens.

Last night, I couldn't sleep either. His screams were harrowing. I don't know what he dreams about, but I do know that not a day goes by where the war does not haunt him. Mom told me that Dad never talked about what he saw, but she found out from his superiors about some of what he went through. She told me about it one drunken night. I do not understand how it is expected for men to lead normal lives after that.

But Dad used to try. Mom said that when I was little, he used to read me stories every night before bed. She told me that he would kiss my forehead and hum lullabies until I fell asleep. He must have done that a long time ago because I do not remember it at all.

For as long as I can remember, Dad has never said much to me. I know that he talks to Mom. I am not sure about what, but they do. Maybe about the weather, maybe about Mom's coworkers, maybe about politics. It's not like I don't spend time with him. Mom works for three days out of the week and for those days, I am at home with Dad. Luckily, Mom works weekends, so I only have to leave school early on Wednesdays. I have my three morning classes and then I skip my last three. It's a one-hour long walk back home. By the time I get here, Dad is usually asleep. I wake him, make him breakfast, brush his teeth, bathe him, put him in different clothes, and supervise him until Mom gets home. It's a lot of time alone with him, yet Dad still feels like a stranger. When the silence between us gets unbearable, I talk to him. I tell him about school, classes, books. Last week, I even told him about Tony. Still, he hardly spares me a glance.

I look a lot like Dad. Mom initially pointed it out to me and now I see it quite often. I share the dark color of his hair and his almond eyes. I have his prominent cheekbones and long eyelashes. Sometimes, it's hard to avoid my resemblance to him. When I look at him I am presented with the inescapable truth. This is the person who created me, the one meant to raise me. I do not blame him for what he went through. I love him. And maybe it's not fair for me to expect anything from him, but I cannot help it. I wish he loved me too.

Mom grabs my arm once she reaches the bottom of the steps. "Where have you been?"

"What?"

"It is seven o'clock, the living room is a mess, the beds aren't made, and you have not even begun preparing dinner. Where have you *been?*"

Was it seven o'clock already? I was at the library with Tony. We did not do anything lewd. He really did help me with schoolwork. I got a lot done. I am still behind, but if I do this for several more days, I can catch up. I can start getting my life together. Before it falls apart again.

Mom smacks the back of my head. I am beginning to miss when the punishments were spankings.

"Last time I checked you could still hear things. Answer me. *Where were you?*" she says furiously.

"I was at the library. I'm behind in school—I need the time to study."

"Were you with Tony?"

"How do you know about Tony?"

"You think that just because Dad doesn't speak to you, he doesn't speak at all?"

Bastard.

"Yes, I was with Tony, but he was helping me"

"You slut."

"Mom, would you just listen to me for a moment? You need to trust me."

"How do you expect me to trust you? You're staying out late with boys and I have to find out about it from *Dad*?"

"Tony is helping me with school! He's going to get my grade up in math. He's really smart!"

"Oh, I'm sure he is. I'm sure he'll be even smarter when you're with him in the back of his car."

I groan in disgust. "I am not talking about this with you." I storm upstairs. She follows me.

"What, Mom?"

She grabs my ear and drags me to my bedroom. "You are going to lower your voice or so help me God, I will ruin your life."

"You already *have*."

"Oh, give me a break. I am not dealing with your nonsense, right now. You are going to go downstairs and you are going to make dinner and then you are going to clean the whole Goddamn house, do you understand me?"

"You're mad. Your whole life is confined to this house and it has driven you insane. And all that insanity gets taken out on *me*. I should have sent you to an asylum years ago!"

She grabs my ear again. She pinches it as hard as she can, like she would rip it off if she could. "I said to keep your voice down."

Just then, Dad enters the room in his wheelchair.

I use this as an opportunity to shove Mom off of me. I turn my attention toward Dad.

"And you. When I make the effort to try to talk to you, you tell Mom? Won't you ever say something *to me*?"

He stares at me sternly. I continue. "Every time I see you, all you have to show me is your resentment. I never wanted to be here. You chose this, you chose to have me! It's not my fault that you won't even bother talking to me. I don't have to do this. I do not have to come home for the rest of my life, worrying about you."

He doesn't say anything.

"Would you speak to me, Goddammit? Would you say something? Anything for Christ's sake!"

Mom slaps a slipper across my face. "Do not speak to your father that way!"

"Oh, what do you know?" I say, rubbing my cheek. Damn, that hurt.

"Excuse me?" she says in disbelief.

I point an accusatory finger at her. "My whole life you have chosen him over me. You forget that I exist, too. I want to be hugged, too."

She scoffs. "You are a woman. Act like it. Getting caught up in childish tomfoolery. Begging me to be hugged. All I did to raise you was useless. You still act like a stupid, naive little girl."

"This isn't stupid."

"Of course it's stupid. Look at yourself, whining about wanting to be hugged in front of your father, a man who has gone through hell for you. I take care of him because he deserves it. You deserve *nothing*. With the way you are acting, you should be on your knees begging for his forgiveness. Begging for mine."

"I do not owe you anything," I say sternly.

"We are your family, you owe me your life."

"You being my family means nothing. For as long as I have been alive I have done everything for you, hoping for an ounce of your love, and still, you treat me like a slave. You do not love me. You do not care about me."

"Don't try to pity yourself," she says. "This is the family you were given, no matter how difficult, you deal with it. And you do not even understand how lucky you are. You have a mom who has given everything so that you will never be reliant on anyone. A dad so noble he went through a war to fight for you to have a life in a country that's not infiltrated by Nazis! You think your life is so *difficult?* You think that I'm such a terrible mom? You would not have been able to live a *day* in mine or your father's life. You do not have the slightest idea what it means for life to be hard. You who cooks dinners, who cleans the beautiful house you live in, who has a mom that works and a dad that cares. You're pathetic. Get back in the kitchen and start cooking dinner. I cannot even look at you."

I have immense respect for Mom and Dad for what they did during the War, but they were not meant to be parents after what they had gone through. This is an endless cycle. Since birth, I have been caged in by my Mom. As time passes by, she continuously shuts my cage a little tighter, making my space to roam a little smaller. Every once in a while, she will remember that she hates me and remind me of my ungratefulness, of my incompetence, my worthlessness. Most times, I haven't done anything in particular, she will have just been drinking again. Always drinking. Glass after glass after glass, like she would be destitute without it. It will kill her some day. And I've decided that I won't be here when it does.

"No. No, I'm leaving."

"You're *leaving*?"

"I cannot do this anymore. I cannot be here anymore."

"You think you can just drop everything and leave? Who do you think you are?"

"I will, you'll see that I will. I'll be in New York City by tomorrow."

"New York City? This is why I never wanted you to rot your mind watching television." She laughs to herself. It's a wretched sound. "It didn't matter, though, in the end. I cannot believe I worked as hard as I did just for my child to end up being someone like you."

I am left speechless. I look at Dad. He is looking back at me this time.

"Nothing to say, Dad?"

Everything about him is sunken. He slouches in his chair, his eyebags sag on his face. But his eyes remain wide. I can see my reflection in his glossy daze.

"I'm sorry," he says, his voice hoarse.

I take a step back. There was a time in my life when I would have given everything to hear his voice. I wondered about his childhood stories. I wished to know his opinions about things—about me. But none of that matters anymore. I don't want to give him the satisfaction of my surprise. I hate him. I hate both of them. I shove my parents out of my room and close the door, barricading it with a vanity chair underneath the doorknob.

I pack all my clothes in my luggage. I shove in everything I think I may need, but I don't take any photos. I am going to make myself forget about this. *If I stay,* I remind myself, *I will be expected to spend the rest of my dad's life coddling him.* Doomed to get by day-by-day, as Mom has been. I don't want that. I don't want to wait for Dad to die until I get to live my life. It's not fair to either of us. Dad hates me. We would be miserable in each other's presence. I want to live somewhere far away. I want to go to the city that everyone speaks so highly of. I want to learn what I desire out of my life and fulfill it. That cannot happen if I don't leave.

I open the door slowly. My clock says that it is four in the morning. I sneak downstairs as stealthily as possible. When I reach the first floor, I shove any canned food in my luggage as well. I try not to think about what I am going to do when I get to New York. All that matters right now is getting there. I take a map and one of the two car keys that are resting inside of a decorative bowl on the living room table. I put on my warmest coat and my best running shoes before I leave the house.

I think about whether I will regret not saying a proper goodbye to my parents, but I do not believe it would matter if I did. Dad has never spoken to me anyway (until today), and I doubt that Mom would care. There is nothing she cares about in this world except for taking care of Dad. No words I could say to Mom will help her understand why I left. My words of closure would be parting words from an apostate to her. I do not want to give Mom something to fuel her resentment. It'll be even easier to hate me once I am gone.

One day, I hope that she regrets this. I hope that she remembers all I did for her. I hope she forgives me for leaving. I hope she forgives herself for making me. My mother, a tortured woman. Such a waste.

I turn on the car's engine and begin pulling out of my driveway. I will never return.

1961

Living in New York has not been unchallenging. When I first arrived, I sold the car and got a job as a dishwasher at a small restaurant in Hell's Kitchen. That was two weeks ago. Since then, I have been saving to rent out a tiny studio apartment in the borough. I do not have the time to go back to high school—so much for all the days I spent trying to learn how to derive a function from a graph. I have had to work so that I can have enough money to pay rent, which will be slightly easier to do when Mr. John F. Kennedy raises the minimum wage in January, bless him. Thus, I improvised my education. The way that I ensure I will not be stuck, chained and enslaved to a husband, is by reading.

I have started reading at least two books a week. I visit the Columbus Library quite often. It has become my place of residence when I am not working. I have read as much as possible, both fiction and nonfiction: philosophy, psychology, romance, art, poems, essays, newspapers, magazines. My favorite book is *Jane Eyre* by Charlotte Brontë. I read it during my first week in the city and nothing I have read since has surpassed its excellence. I love literature, the way words can be woven into stories. The symbolism and beauty that comes along with it. The many ways one singular novel can be interpreted is astounding to me.

Books have been an escape from the reality I am currently facing. I have saved nearly enough money to get my own apartment, but until then, I have been sleeping in the beds of strangers. I am in one right now. In the beginning, I was able to sleep in alleyways, but I realized how much more dangerous that is than if I just...chose someone. Last week, I got desperate. There was a man on the street who clearly took interest in me, and I took advantage of it. As I passed by him, I grazed my hand up his leg and held his hand for an instant. I told him that I would only sleep with him in his apartment, so he took me there. I lost my virginity to him.

It took one more time for it to get easier. I never shared my name, and the man never shared his. I was fine. But the third time, I awoke to a letter of thanks and a fifty-dollar bill. Since then, I have started coming up with fake names. I have given out four so far, and I will give out many more. I am waiting for the day when two familiar men approach me at a bar, and one is greeting me as Cecelia while the other calls me over as Linda.

"Hey...Sylvia-Sue?"

I was feeling creative last night.

"Yes?" I reply softly.

"Make sure you clear out 'fore the wife comes back, all right? I'm goin' to work."

"Yes, of course."

He walks out the door and closes it behind him.

Soon I will have my own apartment. I will begin to look for work as a model. I will sleep with the men I want to sleep with. I will be able to buy things for myself again. Soon I'll prove Mom wrong. Soon.

———————————————————————

Now, I mourn for the childhood that I lost. The fifteen-year-old girl who believed herself to be an adult, thought herself mature enough to give her body away.

As I've grown, I've come to appreciate the newfound empowerment associated with sexual liberty—thank God for the invention of the contraceptive pills—but I was a child then. I was not mature. I did not understand what I was doing, despite how much I insisted that I did. I thought that as long as I was not doing heroin in alleyways, I would be all right. I thought I was being wise for choosing sex over drugs. Someone who was truly wise would know that when presented with a dichotomy of what is acceptable to do, there is always the hidden option of abstinence. Although, you could not tell me that five years ago.

A person does not sincerely understand themselves until they are able to observe themselves in hindsight. Present perception of who you are is altered by the person you want to be. I was young and callow. I wanted to be twenty-five and cunning. I wish I could just tell myself to wait. That time moves past us, whether or not we dwell on the present, so there is no reason to not enjoy it. People spend their entire childhoods yearning to be adults and their entire adulthood yearning to be children once more. It's an error of the human condition.

By the time I was sixteen, I was able to move to a reasonably-sized apartment in Midtown, and I have lived there ever since. After I left home, I was tempted to reach out to my mom. Just because I left did not mean I did not care about my family. There were many nights I stood at a payphone considering whether I should dial. I never did. I always wondered if my mom was in the same position. If she ever made an attempt to call or find me. I think it would be naive to believe that she did.

I can see now that my mom did love me. She tried to raise me to be independent to prevent me from living the life that she did. She just wanted to be appreciated for how hard she worked. I can understand that, and I forgive her, but I never want to see her again.

MEMORY

JUNE 1967

James and I are walking through Central Park, hand-in-hand. Central Park is the perfect place to get lost in your own head. The long, winding roads are boarded with beautiful trees that make you feel like you are not in Manhattan, but rather an enchanting forest. Although I love the vitality of the city, there are moments when the only thing I want is serenity. Several hours ago, I was able to recognize that I was having one of those moments, so I called James. I wanted to escape the chaos of everything. I told him that I wanted to go on a stroll and get ice-cream together. He immediately agreed.

Things have been troublesome with my work lately. It has been difficult to find those willing to hire me. This happens as a freelance model. There are always rough patches. Earlier, I was telling James that it might be time for me to find a steady job somewhere—perhaps as a secretary or a stenographer—to ensure that I do not get evicted in the months to come. Having never gone to college, my selection for jobs is very limited, but James is a massive supporter of my modeling career. He is probably more passionate about it than I am. He wants me to become a supermodel, for every woman to look at me in magazines in awe, the way they do with Jean Shrimpton. I often wonder why James feels this way. Is it what he believes I want, or is it what he wants? There must be glamor in being a supermodel's boyfriend. The woman that people stare at in printed images is the woman he beds. However, I have not told James that I do not love modeling, so he might just support my work the same way that I support his.

I know that James sacrificed a good, steady career for photography. In high school, he excelled in his classes. His mother wanted him to study to become a teacher. He could have done so and been outstanding at it. James has the ability to captivate people when he talks. Students would love him and I know he would share it warmly. But he would never be entirely content knowing that he never attempted to pursue photography.

As a young girl, I wanted to be a living, walking, talking encyclopedia. Every subject, apart from mathematics, fascinated me. Unlike James, I was not a straight-A student. I never had time to do homework and there were certain subjects I was just inherently bad at, but I enjoyed learning. I wanted to know about world affairs, geography, history, anthropology, philosophy. I wanted to read stories—I wanted to be immersed in them. I loved to pretend that their lives were mine. It was my escape from my home, from the reality that awaited me as soon as I opened my front door. I was not a dim child. I understood that my predicament meant that I was not getting an education. That unless I took initiative, I would be trapped in the same fate as many other women—resorting to the life of a hostess to get by. Or worse, I could have become just like my mom.

I chose modeling once I understood that I could not be a woman with a degree in every subject. I told myself that if I wanted to know something, I could read a book. And that is what I have been doing.

Once I progress with modeling, I might make enough money to get some time off. I may return to high school. I could get my GED, go to a liberal arts college. Perhaps I can study psychology. I have always had a deep interest in the mechanics of the mind. How each person's thoughts, reactions, memories, and ideas are so intricate. It is no simple thing. Sometimes, the brain feels separate, like an organ that complies because it wants to—but does not have to. It is a loyal friend that we try to protect, yet when it wounds, it scars all the same. As time passes, you may forget about these scratches, but they linger in the mind.

Sigmund Freud said that there are layers to the human psyche. The way a person presents themselves is not their whole self, even if they are unaware of it. People do not know what they are capable of. The mind is so delicate. So very fickle. How quickly things can change. How easily a person can lose control.

"Penny for your thoughts?" James asks kindly. I look up to realize I have been so distracted that I have forgotten that James has been talking to me.

I shake my head, trying to remove the remaining haziness in my brain. "Pardon me, I didn't mean to ignore you. How was work today?" I ask him.

"Just riveting. One lady ordered a plain black coffee. She was extremely strict about it, said she would have me fired if I made any mistake. Plain. Black. Coffee. I bowed and said a fair, 'Yes ma'am' as I went to get her coffee, right? Then, I returned and placed it on her table and was about to ask if there was anything else I could help her with. She ignored me, inspecting the coffee with such deep interest. She even picked up the cup and looked around it, like she just could not believe I would not mess up a black coffee! I assured her that it was entirely black, not a pinch of sugar or cream in the cup. She looked at me straight in the eyes and told me to leave. I thought it was strange, but I wasn't going to argue—not my problem. You know what she does when I leave?"

"What does she do?"

"Five sugar cubes. Straight into the mug. Five! Can you believe it?" he exasperates, putting his hand up to emphasize just how many five is.

I smile softly.

He frowns in response. "Are you sure that you're all right?"

"Yes, yes. I'm just a little bit tired, that's all," I say.

He looks down at his watch and raises an eyebrow. "At three in the afternoon?"

"Woke up on the wrong side of the bed, I suppose."

He nods. "Ah. Maybe I should start sleeping on the right side and you'll wake up all bright and cheery on the left," he says teasingly. James has had complaints about his side of the bed lately. He says that on the left, the light from the window is inescapable.

"Absolutely not. My body has already adapted to the right side. What if I unknowingly roll around in my sleep? What if I roll in the wrong direction and plop on the floor?"

"We will leave you a pit of leaves to land in softly."

I roll my eyes. "You have clearly never jumped in a pile of leaves. As a child, I nearly sprained both ankles because of it."

He laughs.

"It was not funny, it was very serious, actually! I could have died," I say, but I was laughing too.

"I'm sure, *motek*."

James has begun to use Hebrew pet names for me. *Motek* means sweetheart. Initially, he had refused to, because he knew that I knew nothing about the language. He thought it would be weird calling me things I didn't understand. So, I told him to teach me. I never knew much Italian growing up, only what I learned from kids at school and ladies in supermarkets. I never got the chance to truly be part of my culture. I wanted James to share his with me.

"Also, you are wrong. I used to do that a lot, too, raking the piles of leaves to collapse into. To me, that was the only downside to living in a borough like Manhattan. Everyone's everywhere—can't jump in leaves or build snowmen."

"A valid criticism," I say.

"Oh, of course. Even now I walk down these streets and think, *tsk, where are all the leaf piles? What am I supposed to do with my time now*?"

"Now, you can photograph the new generation of children making those leaf piles. Probably in Central Park, actually."

His smile fades slightly, it is replaced by one that is more solemn, bittersweet. "Ain't that odd?"

I tilt my head slightly. "What's odd?"

He sighs and gestures to his surroundings. "All of this. Watching new kids with their new dads my age. A few days ago, I was talking with this guy at work. Good fellow, somewhere in his early twenties. He asked me about my life, so I asked about his. He told me his wife just had a baby boy that week. I gave him my congratulations and asked what it's like. He said to me, 'I don't know how to explain it. I've only known him for three days, but I just about love the kid more than anything in the damn world.'"

James stares ahead in thought, his blue eyes turning wistful. "You know, when I was a kid, my father would drive me to Manhattan all the time. I used to admire it so much. The lights, the fervor the place ignited in others. You can love a lot about a place you don't spend all your time in. Your imagination fills in the gaps. I grew up in suburban Brooklyn—you know that my family moved there after the war—so I had more chances than not to glorify Manhattan.

"I still loved Brooklyn. It was comfortable. I went to the synagogue with my mother and father every Saturday. I went to school. I rode my bicycle around the neighborhood with my friends and with schoolgirls, and I had a part-time job at an auto shop. My parents were proud of me and my accomplishments. It was the ideal life for a man to have. But there was just nothing quite like when I would visit Manhattan.

"My father and I would drive through the Williamsburg Bridge, my face always against the window as if that could somehow get the photons to reach my eyes faster."

I have no idea what a photon is. I want to ask James to explain it to me, but I would be a fool to interrupt him talking about his childhood. Moments like these are scarce, so I treasure any fact that James shares about his past.

"For my thirteenth birthday, my father gave me his old camera. The Kodak Tourist II with 620mm film. I thought the structure looked funny, like an accordion. I think you would too. You know, I might actually still have it. I can show you when we get home."

I nod. I know what camera he's talking about, I've seen it stowed away in his closet.

"Anyway, he told me that since I was becoming a man, I needed to learn to interpret the world the way I felt right. That's how I would learn what my place in the world is. How to contribute to society, what path to choose. At first, I thought that he was speaking nonsense, an attempt at sentimentality for my Bar Mitzvah. But he said to give it a chance. And that I needed to hurry up because I was making him feel like a movie character sending his son off to manhood. I remember I said to him, with this cheeky grin on my face, 'Is that not precisely what you're doing?' Then he mumbled '*smart Aleck*' to himself and shoved me forward to send me off." James laughs to himself, I smile with him.

"So I did. And I loved it. I took pictures of the Flatiron building, the Empire State building, the Rockefeller Centre, Liberty Island—all of it. My father had to have hated me for having to revisit the same tourist attractions just so I could take a photo only slightly different from the previous. But the times when I had the most fun, when photography truly felt intrinsic to me, were the times when I took photos of people.

"It began with me capturing images of my father, laughing as he watched me cheerfully run around with his camera. And then I started to take photos of strangers walking on the street: their tuxedos and fedoras, their dresses and heels. I loved it. I wanted to move here and do it all the time. Which, evidently, is what I ended up doing.

"I owe it to my father. I would never have picked up a camera, let alone had the motivation to move to Manhattan, were it not for him. I owe everything to him. I loved him, and I know he loved me."

James stops talking for a moment as he reflects. After several seconds, he says, "So I just don't understand why he would do that to himself, why he would do it to me and my mother."

I know about James's father's suicide. David Levins killed himself in 1963 for unknown reasons, but he was reported to be intoxicated before his death. His body was found by an elderly couple the morning after his passing, and they called the police. James was extremely close with his father. I met James two years after the incident, so I didn't see how he handled his grief, and James is not one to divulge—especially with things about himself. I have never pushed James to tell me about what happened. If he ever decided to talk about it, I want it to be on his own accord. It's the least I can do.

"Was he never happy? Are all my memories with him fake? My father was a bona fide man. He valued authenticity and always encouraged me to be honest. How could he be so hypocritical? It's not like I've been thirteen all my life. I've grown. He could have told me if he was depressed, if he felt dejected at home..."

James sighs. "Listen, I love my mother, but she was not the best wife. She did all the housewife tasks with none of the romance. She didn't know any better. Her parents had never been affectionate. Her way of showing love was cooking us hot meals every day. It was all she could do. But I know that my father loved her. He wouldn't have done what he did because of her."

James has stopped walking and is now staring at the floor in anguish. I can feel that he is reliving moments of his life, trying to spot where things changed, what he was missing.

"Was this all my fault? Did he feel lonely after I moved?"

James's father never left Brooklyn. It is only an hour-long drive from James's neighborhood to central Manhattan, where James currently resides. His father could have visited all the time if he or the house were desolate in James's absence. James's father *had* visited him once, two weeks prior to his passing. This could not have been James's fault and he knows it. He just needs to make sense of it, and the only person left to blame is himself. He is not the type of person that would blame his father for his death, and he would never put such a burden on his mother. On the contrary, David's passing brought Elizabeth and James closer together. James calls his mother once a day or two. They talk about their days, the news, their family, and sometimes I hear James talk to her about me. I am glad that however tragic this may have been for James, something good was able to come out of it. I'm sure it is what David would have wanted. Still, it would hurt any father to know how lost his son feels without him.

In James's head, he is the only person that could have caused this.

I wish I could help him, I wish I could give him closure, but I know this is something James will have to solve on his own. I don't need to provide solutions. That is not why he told me all this. He wants me to soothe him. He wants to hear that everything is going to be okay by someone that he can believe means it.

I wrap my arms around him and hug him tightly.

He reciprocates. "Of course it's not your fault, sweetheart. He loved you very much. Nothing will ever change that. Nothing. I promise."

"I don't know how to forgive him," he says through a sob.

As I caress his hair, I realize that I am also crying. I love James. I'm so in love with him. And I hate that he could feel like this. I hate how cruel life can be, how helpless we all are to it and one another. That is a person's blessing and their curse. Your decisions are yours to make, but they will come back to haunt those you love most.

<u>CURRENT</u>

MARCH 1968

"Are you not going to answer me?" James asks.

"I…" I start—but I cannot seem to finish.

You…How could you? I had to, please understand, I needed to. We wouldn't have met—we wouldn't have fallen in love if it were not for me. If it were not for what I did. Could he possibly understand that? James, with all his kindness and careful adoration, would he be able to fathom how I felt?

Heavens, should I have rehearsed for something like this? I had never thought to do so, this did not feel possible, this does not feel real. If my mom could see me right now, she would probably laugh at what I have become. I am not anyone's wife, I am hardly anyone's daughter, I am not even anyone's coworker. The only man who has ever truly loved me is now talking to me like I am hopeless, and it is my fault. I did this. This is the consequence of my actions.

He is my soulmate. James is who I was supposed to meet the very first time. He's who I was supposed to be with forever. He would have listened to me. I could have fixed this.

I know that my silence will not do either of us any good. I gave him his space and now he would like to talk. That means I must respond. I cannot imagine saying anything that would help. I cannot reassure him. I cannot defend myself. I am left to only say how I feel. I think about my mom and whether an explanation would have soothed or infuriated me. I wonder what points she would have emphasized:

"I am sorry for what you dealt with because of me. I wish your childhood was different."

"I planned to be a mom to you—I wanted to style your hair and talk about boys. I wanted to be the one to tell you to be careful around them"

"Your dad was dealt a bad hand and he needed me. I should have never brought you into a family who was not able to care for a child."

I suppose that it's impossible for me to predict how I would feel. It would change depending on when in my life she said it, what my circumstances were, whether I felt forgiving that day. Anyway, it doesn't matter now. Nothing will change. I have already become responsible for saying my own piece to the person I love.

"I never meant to hurt you. I love you...This is not what it was supposed to be."

"What do you mean? How could this have resulted in anything else? I don't know what you were thinking. I don't...How could this be possible?"

Life is a cruel thing. I know it's not fair. Jesus Christ, it's really not fair. James does not deserve this.

James is so giving, so caring. Never jealous, only proud. He is everything I couldn't be and now he suffers for it.

MEMORY

NOVEMBER 1967

I take a long drag of my cigarette while using my other hand to shade the sunlight from my eyes. I hold my breath as I feel the smoke warm my cool lungs, and I slowly exhale. I try not to smoke as often anymore. I did so constantly as a teenager, but now people are saying cigarettes are cancer-causing if you can believe it. But I'm sure a few won't hurt. It's just the perfect weather for one today.

I am taking a walk around the neighborhood. Earlier, I called James to ask if he would like to join me, but the line was busy. I suspect he's on a call with his mother. I'll call him again when I get home.

I stroll freely as I appreciate my surroundings, capturing every glimpse of the gilded city. I love the appearance of Manhattan during autumn. I love the way the leaves' warm colors contrast the chill breeze. It has been a cold week, but today's weather perfectly encapsulates the cozy ambience I associate with the season. Men wear fitted turtlenecks, polo shirts, cardigans and sweaters in various colors with various designs. I've noticed that the popular ones include stripes, polka dots, and different geometric prints. Any shirt that is solid-colored will most likely be in pastels.

Earlier, I saw a man walking down the street with a black button-up sweater with thick red and white stripes that I loved. I may stop by the Gap later and purchase one for James. Women are clothed in woolen long-sleeved dresses, knit sweaters with skirts, and cardigans with slim-fitting trousers in colors of the leaves or of their complementary pairings.

I dressed in a red pullover with crochet trims on my neckline, hem, and collars, accompanied by slim ankle-length pants in the same color. I got it from Darlene, the place on Broadway in South Midtown. It's a lovely little store.

I approach my building and climb the two flights of stairs that it takes to reach my apartment. When I open the door, I am greeted with an unexpected sight.

Seated on my couch is James, his left ankle resting on his right knee, holding a magazine. He is wearing a navy-blue sweater, the precise color of his eyes, with khaki trousers, and smooth black leather slip-ons.

"James, what are you doing here?" I ask. I told him where I hide my spare keys for emergencies, but he seems rather relaxed.

The magazine is one of *Life*'s. The most recent issue. On the cover there are Soviet ballet dancers. They all wear sleeveless pale pink dresses with a silver geometric design paired with elbow-length gloves matched in the color of the dress and silver short-slim heels with a thin buckle. Atop their heads are white bob-cut wigs with bangs. They are beautiful, but *Life* magazine is typically not James's forte. The only magazines I have seen him reading are those of *Aperture* or *U.S. Camera*. He is working toward getting his photos published in either magazine. He has had several in *Modern Photography*, an accomplishment I am extremely proud of him for.

"I decided to pick up a magazine an hour ago," he says flatly.

"I can see that. I didn't know you were interested in *Life* magazine."

"Usually not, no. But I saw a woman reading this issue. She had it opened to the second page, specifically. And I noticed something curious. Would you come here for one moment?"

I slowly approach him.

He angles the magazine page toward me so I can get a better look. Now I understand. Printed on the flimsy paper are three photos of me. In them, I am wearing a long, pink silk dress. It is strapless and tight around my waist. To enhance the look, I have on white elbow-length gloves and a bold, chunky diamond necklace. My hair is neatly curled and firm. Absolutely unmovable. That day, I remember being increasingly frightened as the hairdressers relentlessly applied hairspray and gels to my hair. It was a nightmare to wash out. I might have spent an hour in the shower scrubbing out all the stubborn chemicals alone.

In the first photo, I am simply posing for the camera. I am leaning on a wooden stool with my right arm. Only I and the stool are in front of the plain black background. In the second image, I am significantly closer to the camera, and I am leaning forward slightly, highlighting the glistening diamonds on my neck. There is a man, appearing to be my husband, in a navy-blue suit with a tie the color of the red carnation in his mouth. He is standing behind me with one leg behind the other, his head tilted slightly, as if expecting me to turn around so he can surprise me. The final photo frames our faces. My chin is angled toward the man while he kisses my temple from behind. My widened eyes look ahead, past the camera and my mouth is slightly agape in pretend delighted shock. Only the right side of his face is visible—one deep brown eye, black gelled hair, a straight nose, a shaved beard. It was enough to see that he was a very handsome man indeed. Is that what James is angry about? The depiction of me with another man?

Before I can ask him about it, he leaps from the couch, lifts me in his arms and spins me around.

"How could you not tell me that you're in a magazine as large as *Life?* I would have brought you jewelry or flowers, anything to celebrate! Hopefully you don't want the necklace that you're wearing in those photos, that might be a bit beyond my budget. Though, I can always use my rent money."

He puts me down with a grin though I'm still a little bit bewildered. "You're not upset?"

"Upset? Why would I be upset?"

"Because of the man in the photo."

"The actor?" He laughs. It's such a wonderful sound. "Of course I'm not upset! Though, next time this happens, tell me. I don't want to find out from some lady on the street. I want you to come home and tell me so I can go to the florist as soon as possible. Can you believe I'm empty-handed? You have your photo taken for *Life* and I don't have flowers to give you. Maybe you're right, maybe I should be upset."

I smile at him in awe before I lean in to kiss him. The kiss is not extremely passionate or lascivious. It's delicate. He reciprocates while pressing his hands into my lower back. He kisses me slowly to make me feel appreciated. He continues to kiss me deeply as he leads me toward the bedroom. I follow willingly.

Now, we lay in bed together, my head resting on his bicep while James mindlessly strokes my hair.

The faint sounds of New York City accompany the breeze that enters from the slightly opened window. Our clothes lay discarded on James's bedroom floor. I need to check to see if all the stitches remain sewn in my pants later. My hand caresses his chest. James is muscular—not so much that his chest feels like a rock, yet enough to be a striking sight in every woman's peripheral vision. When we walk down the street together, I discern that I am not the only one who believes James is a sight for sore eyes. I am not sure I would consider myself the jealous type. I do care, but I also know that while women yearn for James's to meet their eyes, his are already on mine.

Excuse my lack of modesty, but I am a beautiful woman—I would not have been able to model otherwise. I know that James believes that he is special for being the man currently next to me. It's flattering. Even though James knows my first time was not with him, he still treats sex as sacred. He was the first person who showed me that sex did not have to be unlawful or lewd. James touches me to make love to me.

Before James, there were only one or two men that I slept with because I wanted to. Most of the time, if I did not need to, I did not accept the advances I received. I made sure I knew how to reject politely and leave immediately. The world is a dangerous place for a woman who does not know how to make a man feel desired even when he is being pardoned. However, to sleep with just any man is incomparable to being with James. I have learned enough about myself to understand what I need to take from men for my pleasure. With James I don't need to take, he gives freely.

I loll my head up toward him. "I love your eyes," I whisper.

He looks down at me, mockingly imitating a seductive glare. "Is that so?"

I laugh and playfully shove him away, but he instantly reels me back in. His strong arms wrap around my torso. I look back into his eyes. We take a moment then, just looking at each other.

I mindlessly reach my arm up to caress the line of his jaw, slightly softened because of his position on the bed. His face is composed of features that mesmerize my wandering eyes. The freckles of stars, the dimples when he smiles, the fullness of his lips.

"Beautiful," I whisper.

He kisses me softly and returns his fingers to my hair. He doesn't say anything after that. I don't think he needs to.

MEMORY

JANUARY 1968

I am humming mindlessly, attempting to fix James's record player, when I hear him walk toward the room behind me. The record player, typically residing beside the doorframe of the bedroom, has been moved to accompany James's nightstand after he nearly broke it walking out of his room.

Sometimes, James does this thing where he leans against the doorframe, waiting to make an appearance on his own terms. I once asked him about it and he told me his father taught him to do so, that it would "bring the ladies to their knees." To indulge him, I went straight to my knees. He laughed and brought me down to my back while he settled on top of me.

I can feel James's presence behind me, his arm resting against the doorframe. However, I am very set on fixing this record player right now. James and I have made a regular habit of dancing together. Every other week, usually at the end of the day, he lets me choose any record and we dance in the middle of the apartment while the vinyl spins. It has become something I look forward to. I am perpetually swooning when he holds me in his arms.

When we are not dancing, James looks through his collection of records and lets one play in the background of our lives. Most of the time, it's The Beach Boys. I feel like I have become more familiar with Brian Wilson's voice than my own.

As I fiddle with the stylus, I start to mumble the lyrics to "Jesus Wash Away My Troubles" by Sam Cooke. I suppose from an outsider's perspective, seeing a woman kneeling and muttering Jesus' name periodically would appear to be quite different from what is currently happening.

James shifts in position, believing he has intruded on my time with God. "I'm sorry, I didn't know you prayed. I wouldn't have interrupted."

I respond but do not turn around, restraining my laughter. "No, darling, I was just singing a song."

I hadn't even been thinking about what the lyrics mean, I really do just like Sam Cooke. Earlier, I had been listening to "Bring It On Home To Me." When Sam's voice began distorting, I realized there was an issue with the record player. Now here we are.

"I came in here to ask if you would like some coffee," he says. "Chock Full o' Nuts has been rather busy and frankly, I don't feel like being there as a customer. I love Earl like an uncle, but with all the rush he would probably send my 'ass back to work.' And anyway, I think it would be nice if we made it here, just the two of us."

I turn around so that I can look at him. I notice that he's cleaned himself up. His hair is gelled and combed back. He wears fitted black trousers with a white cotton turtleneck. His black overcoat is draped on his arm.

"That would be lovely. Thank you, honey."

He seems to relax knowing that I wasn't praying, that he didn't interfere with anything. He smiles and leaves.

James Levins is a proud Jewish man. It has never bothered him that I grew up Catholic. During December, we celebrate both our cultures. We light the menorah for eight nights, and I listen to his prayers and his childhood stories of competitive dreidel battles for chocolate coins. I love how passionate he is about his culture, and I love how he shines when he shares it with me.

I have never been very religious. I keep that fact very private with other people. It is not uncommon to correlate lack of faith with lack of humanity, but James never minded. Still, last year, we lit a Christmas tree together. That same year, James surprised me by coming to my apartment after drunkenly dressing up as Santa Claus at a work Christmas party. It would have been funny if it had not been midnight and I didn't think that a burglar had just broken into my home.

I begin to realize that I may just have to buy James a new record player when he informs me that the coffee is ready. I leave the stylus I have been fiddling with and enter the living room. On the television, Audrey Hepburn sings "Moon River" as George Peppard gazes at her fondly from above. It makes me think about watching *Roman Holiday* as a young girl. Enamored by a television screen for the first time.

I would never have admitted it then—I was at the peak of the severe teenage rebellious phase I had entered, believing it was the first step to adulthood—but when I slept with all those men, I secretly hoped one would discover something in me, something beyond my sexuality, and choose to stay. I thought love could happen in a single night, like it does in the films. Now, I don't know about the world of cinema, but in reality, love takes time. Love takes learning about the person. A few years ago, I nearly gave up on the whole concept. I thought that maybe I was incapable of it. But then came James.

Even now it feels childish to talk about such things because it feels so idealistic. A man who loves you the way James does is not an easy thing to find. James's love for me is credited to his sentimentality. It's probably because he's an artist. Nevertheless, I love each aspect of him equally and immeasurably. Every time I am with James, I understand what I had been yearning for all those years. I see why all anyone ever talks about is romance. I understand that each person falling in love feels like they are the only one who has ever felt it before. It is one of the only things in life that is so unoriginal, yet so personally special. All those films about eternal devotion, or about the intertwining

of two people into one soul—they still do not amount
to the ardor one feels while in love.

If you have not yet loved a person, then do not rely
on anything to depict what it will be like. Sure, as a girl
I too wanted my own Joe Bradley, but James is not Joe
Bradley. He is much more profound. Love and hatred
are the two emotions that cannot be written and
cannot be expressed unless felt. I've taken an interest in
expressionistic art lately because of that. The fact that
visuals can evoke emotion that words at times cannot.
Still, it is impossible to endure all the sensations the
artist did while painting or drawing, impossible to
completely understand actions taken for love when
you have not experienced it at all.

James is standing behind the kitchen counter,
steaming coffee in one hand, flowers in the other, with
my favorite date-bread and cream cheese sandwich
from Chock Full o' Nuts on the counter.

My walking slows. "What's all this?"

"I wanted to surprise you." James has the brightest
expression on his face.

"Well, you did!" I say in awe. "Thank you, my
dear." I walk up and kiss him. I take the flowers and fill
the vase that has been sitting empty with water. James
sets the coffee down, and I sit at the tall chair in front
of the counter. I take the first bite of the sandwich and
look at him with a hand to my chest, expressing my
immense gratitude to him for granting me such an
experience. He smiles and fidgets with his fingernails.
He looks uncomfortable. No, that's not it. He's

nervous. Really nervous. James has been anxious before, everyone has, but right now he is trying to cover up his shaking hands. This is not normal.

I make sure to swallow before I speak. It will not help if he has to witness the half-digested food in my mouth before saying what he needs to say.

"James, is everything all right? You're trembling."

He looks at me, the sunlight entering through the window is making his gilded eyelashes glisten. "I want to talk to you about something. Something important, before I ask you properly."

"Ah, was all this just to butter me up?"

His eyes squint nervously. "I hope not?"

"Okay..."

He wants to talk to me about something before asking me another thing. Oh, Christ. What a terrible time to have admitted I am not religious. I just burned bridges with the only person who could have helped me here.

Perhaps I am wrong. Perhaps James just wants to take a trip together and is worried it will interfere with our jobs!

"I think we should get married," he says.

Of course I'm not wrong. I'm never wrong.

"James..."

Of course I have thought about it before. Everyone I know—which, granted, is not that many people—is married or engaged. I love James, and these past three years have been the best of my life, but marriage horrifies me. I do not want James to wield the power that a man has as a husband. I do not want to be reduced to a wife, my tasks strictly consisting of mindless chores. And with marriage comes motherhood, a role I am not capable of fulfilling.

I hope for James to understand what my response insinuates and to kiss me and tell me that it's okay if I don't ever want to get married. That we will live happily together forever as boyfriend and girlfriend. He doesn't do that. He waits patiently for my answer. He knows what it will be, but he has the habit of breaking his own heart. He needs to hear the words. And I can't bring myself to say them.

"I don't think that it's the right time. We will, I promise, just give it some while longer."

This is the first real lie I have told James and I do not understand why I even did so. Am I that afraid that he is going to leave me for another woman? There are plenty of women who would switch places with me instantaneously. Many women who are more than willing to give James what I cannot. Do I need him that badly? So much so that I lie about who I am, about what my beliefs are? As I ask myself these things I notice that I have no intention of telling him any of it. This is how I am choosing to handle the situation, by lying to him.

I can see that James is disappointed. I know this is not how he envisioned this would go. But James Levins has never been one to give up so easily.

"When?" he asks.

"What?" I say, startled.

"When would you want to marry?" he specifies.

"Oh, I don't know, in a few years."

"A *few* years?" he questions.

How much longer do I think is a reasonable amount of time for him to possibly change his mind?

"Four?" I suggest hesitantly.

"*Four?*" he exasperates.

"Three?" I offer.

He tries to brighten his demeanor to make me see things from his perspective. How happy we would be as husband and wife.

"Listen, please—there is no reason to be uncertain, the wedding would be wonderful. You can buy any wedding dress you like. Whether you are wearing something extravagant or a cardboard box, I will marry you with glee. I want to grow old with you. I want to photograph you for the rest of our lives. I want your life to be timeless. People will look at your pictures and see the difference between being captured by some random photographer and by the man who adores you. I know you intimately. I want you to see yourself encapsulated in an image that shows that, for you to forever see yourself the way I do. And the wedding itself, to compliment your beauty, will be artistry. Of course, there will be flowers, such beautiful flowers— dahlias, chrysanthemums, roses, tulips, daffodils, hyacinths. Anything, anything at all."

I don't even know what half of those flowers are. And I am beginning to realize that James does not give me pre-made bouquets, he deliberately chooses each individual flower to incorporate. Oh, what an extraordinary man James Levins is. It hurts me to do this to him. I am the one making him plead for his happiness. I am the person telling him that he cannot marry the woman he loves. My gaze turns sullen, but he ignores it.

"And—And we'll invite both our families...or just mine. At the very least you must meet my mother! She has been consistently asking about you. I don't know what to tell her anymore, how to delay your visit any longer. I know you said you're not comfortable with it because of what your parents were like. I wish you would talk to me about that, by the way. I know you're not being completely honest with me. A husband should know about things like this. I know we're not married yet, that's why I haven't mentioned it, but I want to be able to help you. I can't help you if you don't tell me things.

"Even still, you're my girlfriend, I want you to meet my mother. She means a lot to me, and she deserves to know who the woman I love is. And you don't have to worry, she'll love you! I talk about you all the time, so you already have a good reputation. This will be a celebration, I promise."

James is right about one thing—he does not properly know about my family. He once asked me why I never talk about them, if I ever call them. I told him that I had not called them in a long time, that they were very difficult when I moved out, that they did not make my childhood easy for me. I did not lie to him—I just did not tell him all the details. He didn't need to know. I was going to tell him the whole truth eventually, that I vowed to never interact with my family again, but why now? Why must I tell him things if I don't feel ready to yet? Why do we have to follow expectations for our relationship? Why can't we be young and in love for a little bit longer?

James continues, "If you want to do it in the future, then why not do it now?"

"Could I not ask you the same? What is the point of caging ourselves into marriage right now? I love you and you love me, isn't that enough?"

"Why do you think of marriage like that? Marriage doesn't have to be imprisonment. Marriage can be romantic. I can give that to you every day for the rest of our lives. We can start a family together, you and I," he says earnestly.

I should not have lied. All I have done is delay the inevitable rebirth of why I left Connecticut in the first place. Is this what I am fated for?

"James, could we please not do this?"

"I want to do this. I want to argue with you about this. I want to devote myself to you completely. I want everything I have to be ours. I want this for the rest of my life." He sighs. "Do you not want that, too?"

I want to say that I never planned to marry, that I can cherish our relationship without getting any government documents involved, without a signature constricting me to it. I know that James would never intentionally make me feel subjected to him. I know that he wants to use marriage as a declaration of his love for me. But I also don't want James to eventually feel subjected to me. Eventually, marriage gets tough and then it is not about romance anymore. Sometimes you are forced into situations that test your vigor, sometimes your husband feels like he is obligated to love you, sometimes you end up like my mom and dad. I am not willing to risk that. I am going to tell him that I'm not sacrificing my beliefs for anyone, even him. That if this relationship is going to work, he will have to respect that.

When I open my mouth, my words disobey me. "Oh, James, of course I want this. I want to spend all of my time with you. I just want that stage of our lives to come a little later. If we know we want to be together, then what's the rush?"

He frowns. I know that he had a day planned to celebrate. He might have even been planning on proposing today. There could be an engagement ring in his pocket right now. James closes his eyes. I am prepared for him to lose it. Maybe he'll finally yell at me or accuse me of wanting to sleep with other men, of not truly loving him.

He takes a deep breath, suppressing his anger, and says, "Okay."

I know him better than this. This is not one of those moments where he takes my side. He is letting me have my way now so that he can subtly convince me to get married over the next few weeks. I am not going to change my mind.

I am about to get up to kiss him and apologize, but he simply walks past me. "I'm going to fix the record player," he says.

What have I done?

CURRENT

MARCH 1968

"I pictured a life with you. Nothing was ever supposed to come in the way of that. Truly, *truly*," I say.

His dirty-blonde hair has become disheveled. He stopped applying gel to it the day after I told him I preferred it natural. He has run his fingers through and tugged his thin waves enough to ruin its natural flow. His dark blue eyes, once passionate, are now forlorn. My lover stands here, before me, like a child who has lost his toy. I feel helpless.

Hatred is an easy emotion to resort to. When a person has any antipathy towards us, we feel a natural impulse to reciprocate it. It is normal to hold a grudge when you feel slighted. I cannot bring myself to feel that way about James Levins. Oh, how I gravitate toward him. Despite the circumstances, I am not scared of him because I know that I am just witnessing him *feeling*. Sometimes emotion can be overwhelming to him and just watching him navigate it feels sacred to me. Everything he feels I want to feel tenfold. I hate that his current feelings complicate that.

I can see that he feels troubled, too. Two sides of his conscience battle for a chance to speak, to act. He is considering what to do with me. He is wondering what he wants from me. How this is going to end. How far he can go. How much I'll allow. How much he will allow himself. Morals become complicated when you no longer want to obey them.

"What do you expect me to do?" he asks.

I sigh. "I feel like I should be the one asking that question."

"You're not. You're hardly saying a word. Your only explanations have been empty apologies."

"James—"

"What?"

I pause.

"No, tell me. This whole time I have been standing here waiting for you to say something. To *actually* say something," he says, raising his voice.

I am not getting out of this the way I wish I could. One way or another, I will have to talk. But, at the very least, I want to warn him. "No matter what I say, it'll upset you. This has no chance of ending well."

"So *now* we're considerate of each other's feelings? This is ridiculous. For the love of God, would you just start fucking speaking?"

I take a step back. "It's not ridiculous. I don't want to hurt you."

He puts his face in his hands.

"James, I mean it."

"Sure, right. You mean it."

He crosses his arms and sighs. "Fine, okay. Let me be straight with you, since you're too much of a coward to do so yourself."

That hurt.

"I do not care whether or not you want to hurt me," he says. "I do not care whether or not you are hurt. I have only asked you one thing, and how kind of me to only *ask*."

"I understand that you're going to be angry and you have every right to b—"

"*Enough!*" he screams. "Just tell me."

I have never seen James like this before. I've never heard his words so malevolent. I wonder where this version of him has been hiding. Or whether it has been hiding at all. I have seen James at his most vulnerable— talking about his father, making love, making art. And I thought that was his most authentic self. I cannot say that this is not him as well. This is just another side of him, another reaction to another vulnerable situation. Every moment I have spent with James has been *him*. Just because this is not preferable does not mean it's not James. And I will not vilify him for it.

I take a deep breath. "Okay."

MEMORY

I have just finished cooking dinner for James and I. A platter of salmon, brussels sprouts, and fresh-baked dilly bread lays on the table.

I know I am not the best cook, but I think my meals suffice. They are well-balanced and nutritious. However repetitive and mundane my cooking gets, I will never serve my boyfriend any of that gelatinous rubbish that I have been spotting in cookbooks again. First of all, if I did, he would leave me. Second, I am not cooking for my parents anymore. The food I make is either consumed by me or the man I love, so why in the world would I ever feed us such a contraption? I know that people began eating meals in Jell-o after the war from girls at school. It was convenient and had a longer shelf-life. I did not understand the meals-in-a-mold craze and by the time I had grown up, it was gone anyway.

However, it was brought up again several days ago. A fellow model and I were chatting in our trailer. She is an older woman, somewhere in her mid-forties. I was solidifying my now collarbone-length puffed hair with incredible quantities of hairspray. I had my hair cut into bangs—a horrendous decision, I was in fear of losing my job—and I was trying to find a way to make it work. I could not prepare the scheduled hairstyle with my new haircut, so I settled for a low beehive updo with bangs. When in doubt, mimic a hairstyle from another model. Thank you, Brigette Bardot.

Anyway, as the model discussed her day, she mentioned that she had read a recipe in a weight watchers cookbook that she owned. This woman was petite, keep in mind. She only had curves because of her bosom and behind. It was nothing dire, unlike the recipe—sliced up liver and green beans were jellified using chicken stock as a base and drizzled with a buttermilk gelatin glaze. I had to withhold my gag as I heard it. She told me that it is called Liver Pâté en Masque. The name being in French was clearly an attempt to mask the atrocity of it. Yet that was not all. The Liver Pâté En Masque was only her central dish— her accompanying side dishes were chicken mousse and coleslaw in a mold. That poor family of hers.

The day before, I had felt fancy and decided to try a recipe from a cookbook James had laying around. He said his mother had given it to him after he moved in, scared that without a woman in the house, he wouldn't know what to cook and would starve. It was a meatloaf with some Campbell's condensed tomato soup. The recipe said to add American cheese on top, but James does not mix meat and dairy.

When I told the model about this meal, she said, "That's neat. What about the side dishes?"

I furrowed my eyebrows. "Side dishes?" I asked. James and I could hardly finish the meatloaf.

She looked at me aghast and replied, "Oh, darling, do you not prepare side dishes? You must! I have this incredible Jell-O garden salad recipe I can bring for you."

It sounded like a meal so terrible it would be inhumane to feed it to criminals. But with all the kindness I could muster, I said, "Oh, you are a dear but I mustn't. My boyfriend cannot eat gelatin, he's...kosher." Using his practice as an excuse to politely reject her offer.

I could not see James that day so I called him on the telephone the next morning and told him about it. James, typically as chivalrous as it gets, replied to my description of her suppers with, "Is she *mad*?"

James is now rolling up his sleeves, preparing to eat. I ate earlier and could not bring myself to eat again. I apologized to him for not saving my appetite and he told me that he was thankful I took the time to make dinner at all.

I scrub the dishes I used to prepare the food. James offered to do it himself after he finished eating, but I cannot stand having dishes left in the sink, especially when they reek of fish. Also, as sweet as he is to offer, James is terrible at washing dishes. He can't handle the temperature the water needs to be at for sanitation. He has accused me of trying to give him second degree burns by turning up the heat. Thus, the food residue never gets washed off properly, and we are back where we started.

"James, I overheard the most curious thing at work today."

"Lay it on me," he says.

"You know Carol? The English model that walked the runway with me a couple of months ago?"

"The one who you caught with the coke in the bathroom?"

I nod. The industry isn't perfect. A lot of the girls use it for weight loss, along with Obetrol. I avoid the pills by skipping out on breakfast and dessert.

"What about her?"

"You know that she's married."

He glances up at me for an instant before returning his gaze to his plate, picking at his food with his fork. "Sure."

Ever since our conversation about marriage a month ago, things have been different. Not so different that anyone apart from James and I could recognize it—last week he visited me at work which evoked a "Aren't you two just the sweetest things? I can't wait for the wedding!" from the receptionist of the building—but it lingers between the two of us like an undiscovered force. I wouldn't go as far as to say that James has been distant, but it almost feels like all his acts of affection are compulsory. Perhaps I am being dramatic. I have been treating him like nothing happened, like everything is how it's always been. Something just feels strange.

"I heard that she had an affair," I say. "But it's a real quiet thing, no one knows apparently."

"Oh?"

"With their milkman."

"The milkman?" he repeats, eyes wide in shock.

"Supposedly, he's a handsome fellow. A real Marlon Brando type."

He raises an eyebrow. "Their milkman resembles Marlon Brando? *Really*?" He draws out the "really" to emphasize his point.

I take a second to think about it. "Okay, this may not be the most accurate information."

"You think?" he asks teasingly.

"Hey, don't shoot the messenger. This is only what I heard."

James smiles at that. "Well, handsome fellow or not, it's infidelity. It's demeaning to that husband of hers." Then he says, under his breath, "Especially with the Goddamn milkman. Poor bastard."

"Well, of course, but you do not know what her marriage was like." I shrug.

He pauses eating. "What are you implying—that she's not a whore?"

I shrug lightly. "I think that nothing is so simple."

He looks at me skeptically. "What complicates it?"

"We don't know their marriage. What if her husband were hitting her, or neglecting her?"

"In that case, you would be right. She's not a whore, *rak mefagerette,*" he says before taking another bite of his salmon.

I have spent enough time with James to pick up on a little bit of Hebrew—even though he too doesn't know many words himself, mostly curses he learned from his mother or terms of endearment he learned from his father. What he just said translates to, "she's not a whore, only retarded."

"James, don't be so obtuse."

"Sorry, I just think it's unacceptable under any circumstance. Not to mention, she might just be risking something way worse with her husband. That is not to say that I'm condoning it, a man should never lay a finger on a woman, but if you're not happy, then divorce. It benefits both parties of the relationship." He stabs his fork into a singular brussels sprout and plops it into his mouth.

It is moments like these that remind me that, although I love James like he is part of my brain and body, we are different people. Firstly, he is a man. Don't get me mistaken, he is more open-minded than anyone I have ever met. Several months ago, I heard James in an argument with his mother after she gossiped to him about his cousin's secret abortion. He was yelling at her, "If Aviva can't afford to have the baby, then why should she? I don't understand your problem. No—no—Why shouldn't she get rid of her own pregnancy? And stop telling the whole family about it. Not only does it make you look bad, but

Aviva does not need this right now." Terrible situation for Aviva, but I had never been so attracted to a man in my life. When he got off the phone, I practically pounced on him.

Nevertheless, James is a man, and he will never completely understand some things. For example, divorce is not simple. Lately, it has become much easier to divorce as a woman, thank God, but there is still a ways to go. Many people are still stuck in the mindset that marriage is an obligation to another person. Especially from a wife to a husband. He does not understand the pressure a woman faces to stay in her marriage.

I do not say anything in response to him and he notices.

"What bothers you about what I said?" he asks.

"I'm not bothered."

He raises an eyebrow, displaying his doubt.

"What? It's your opinion. I cannot dissent," I say.

"You can resent."

I roll my eyes. "Okay, Dr. Seuss."

"You know that I didn't mean to rhyme. But really, why's this bug you so much? Was it my use of the term 'whore'? Fine, you're right, I'll refrain from it."

"Well, good, I'm glad, but it was not distinctly that which bothered me."

He waits patiently for me to continue.

"It's just that you always see things in absolutes. She is either a whore or a devoted wife."

He sighs. "This again? I can't apologize over and over for the way I think. I love that you want everyone to be a little good, I think it's sweet, but it's not the world works. And you know what, honey? I hope you never encounter a person so deplorable that you ever agree with me."

He has finished with his meal and is bringing his plate to the sink. He softly cradles my chin and leans in to kiss me, but I stop him.

"You smell like fish."

He gasps in exaggerated disbelief. "Whoa, suddenly the girl from Connecticut has problems with fish?"

"I've lived here for six years. I could be starting to adapt."

"Mhm, sure," he says and kisses my forehead instead. "I'm going to go brush my teeth and shower now that you have left me feeling undesired." He dramatically slams a hand to his heart like he has been stabbed. Or at least he attempts to. For a man who can dance so beautifully, James is very uncoordinated. His hand lands above his heart, it appears as if he has been dreadfully stabbed in the shoulder.

"Go shower, fish boy. An animal needs to be in its habitat"

His jaw falls agape. "*Chutzpah*!" he calls to me as he makes his way toward the bathroom. An accusatory "rude!"

I smile for a moment, but it fades. James left on purpose. He knows how to avoid arguments that he does not think are worth having. And I guess that is what upsets me this time—how stubborn he is about this. I know that it is not fair for me to feel this way, yet I cannot help to be aggravated by it. I suppose that I thought I would be able to convince him to see my side of things. He has listened to me. We have talked about this numerous times before, but he does not change. He is set on categories. Good or bad, black or white, cats or dogs. He hates cats, by the way, apparently has only ever loved dogs. He never had one growing up because he's allergic, but any time we pass a dog in the street, he pets it. A few weeks ago, he stopped in the middle of 42nd street to pet a stranger's beagle. He sneezed for two days straight. I like dogs, but I prefer cats. I wouldn't mind sitting in Central Park with a book in one hand and a cat in the other. I asked James if we could get a pet once, any pet, to which he informed he was allergic to all animal hair. What a bummer, I think we would have made excellent pet owners.

Though it seems to me that James would protest against us getting a pet. He would mention marriage again—ask why we don't just have a baby instead. He would argue, "A combination of ourselves would be fantastic. Children give life a meaning greater than any career or monetary item." And I would reply, "James, I would love to have a child with you. When I'm older. When all the wrinkles I would get will have already become unavoidable." Which is true. I am doomed to be old, why hasten the process with pregnancy? And anyway, I am not fit to be a mother. I have already raised myself all my life. My only daughter is already twenty-one years old. I cannot raise another. I will not spend another two decades nurturing and teaching. Don't I deserve a childhood of my own?

Not James, though. James had a childhood with a father to guide him the whole time. A father he loved and cherished. James would make a wonderful dad. He wants to replicate the experience he had with his father—I want to pretend mine never existed.

If my dad died, I don't think I would even be informed of it. There is a chance he may be dead right now. I know it may seem like a terrible thing to say, but for the health of both my parents, I do hope he has come to rest.

Approximately fifteen minutes pass before I hear the water turn off. James walks out with wet hair and a towel wrapped around his waist.

"Don't you look handsome."

"Wasn't I just 'fish boy' to you?" he questions teasingly.

"Forgive me?" I say as I walk toward him, already knowing where this will lead. He indulges me at first, kissing me slowly.

"I have to be up early tomorrow," he says when our lips separate.

"That's not a problem. It'll be quick." I kiss him again, but he breaks it.

"I should sleep, dear. Let's both sleep early tonight. Have you finished cleaning up?"

"Nearly," I say disappointedly.

"Whatever you need to do now, I will do tomorrow, okay?"

"Sure. I'll meet you in bed, I want to shower first."

"All right." He kisses me and then returns to the room while I follow behind, turning to enter the bathroom.

I try not to get upset with James. I just need a moment to myself. I turn on the water for the shower and wait as it warms. I strip myself of my clothes and catch sight of my body in the mirror. I have never gotten used to seeing myself naked. My perception of it has changed drastically throughout my life. As a girl, I felt that my youthful body did not belong to me, that it had not caught up with my maturity.

My first period felt like a joke. I found out about menstruation when I was ten. My mom had fleetingly mentioned that when I started bleeding from my "private place," there were sanitary pads hidden beneath the sink that would absorb the blood. When I asked why I would start bleeding at all, she told me, "It means you're a woman and...capable of bearing a child. So long as you're not whoring around, you'll be fine."

I got it two years later. It was like my body announcing that it had finally reached where I was in my life—look at me, I'm a woman too!

As I stare at myself now, I feel the exact opposite of how I did when I was twelve. This is the body of a lady, and I still feel like a girl. My breasts are small but visible, my bottom larger and curvier. My hips protrude while my waist narrows. I cannot identify when it happened. I feel like I am constantly watching myself in the perspective of another person, the mirror of a distant relative greeting you with, "Look how much you've grown! Where does the time go?"

I want to revert to what once was. I am not ready yet. I cannot bear a child. I need to be held. I need to be reassured. I need to be protected.

I step into the tub and close the curtain. The water spills onto my head and warms my body. My head spins. *Pull yourself together,* it tells me. But I cannot seem to any longer. I'm not in control.

I sit down on the floor, and I cry like I haven't done since I was fifteen.

MEMORY

MARCH 1968

"I can't find it!" James calls from my bedroom. "You've got a lot in here. I thought that you were organized, this is a new side of you I'm seeing," I hear him mumble to himself.

"Keep searching, it should be there. I know it's a bit of a mess, but it should not be that hard to spot!"

I sent him to fetch a faux-pearl necklace from my vanity drawer, one that would perfectly complement my black cocktail dress. I have my hair worn down, treated with hairspray to make it appear voluminous. My bangs fall smoothly over my eyebrows. I applied a light layer of white eyeshadow, with a thick swoop of eyeliner, nude lipstick, and false eyelashes.

I am meeting James's mother tonight. James only informed me this morning that last week, Elizabeth scheduled a date for us to visit, begging for us to come. Supposedly, she has already prepared us supper and dessert, so there is no opportunity to cancel. I was furious that James went behind my back and agreed on both of our behalf. But truthfully, I am surprised that he did not do this sooner. He waited for me to feel comfortable, waited for me to want to do this. I suppose he knows better than that by now.

Upon his request, I dressed James. He has several colorful suits, and he had planned to wear his eggshell blue one, but I was told that his mother is a conservative woman, and I did not think she would appreciate such a color. Thus, I selected a thinly plaided dark gray one with a burgundy tie. When I provided the suggestion, James guaranteed that his mother would judge him anyway for wearing an outfit he has had since he was twenty. I told him that I doubt that she remembers a suit he wore five years ago, especially with how infrequently he has seen her since. He replied, "When you meet her, it will all make sense."

James has not cut his hair in three months. It has grown out of his usual messy side part and into miniature bangs with shaggy sides. It is not so long that he appears unkempt, but enough so that his hair curls delicately at the ends. He may decide to gel his hair for Elizabeth.

Today is extremely important to James. I know how much it means to him that I meet his mother. I do not know how this meeting could go well for me either way. His mother is very traditional. She would want us wed by next week if she likes me or separated by tonight if she doesn't. Perhaps I shall make her hate me. James will resent her for doing so and then we can remove her from our lives, or at least mine. There is nothing less I want than to meet Elizabeth Levins.

I open the fridge, considering drinking a glass of wine to loosen up. Possibly two glasses. I take the bottle of red wine out and pour myself some. As I sip from the glass, several droplets of wine fall onto my chest.

"God dammit!" I shriek.

I place the wine back on the countertop and I take a deep breath. Great. This is just great.

"James, honey, have you found the necklace?"

I begin to walk toward my room.

"You may not need to anymore. I wanted to have a glass of wine before we left and I spilled some on my dress. I am not sure if it's noticeable. I need you to check and let me know. If anything, I can wear another dress so there's no need to worry! Although, that means we probably need to find a different necklace, the pearls might not work."

I walk in, and James's back faces me.

"Sweetheart, did you hear me?"

"What's this?" he asks flatly.

All thoughts of the wine evade my mind. My stomach drops as I see that James is not searching through my vanity drawer but the bottom drawer on my nightstand. He has taken out a stack of years-old magazines, discarded pens, and cigarettes. I have not opened that drawer in years. I let myself pretend it was not there. I cannot believe that I let myself become so reckless.

"What's what?" I say innocently. I feel my lungs fill up with sand.

He is hovering over the empty drawer with his head hanging down. I have never seen a person stand so still. I take one step toward him. I do not want to look at what he's holding. I do not want to be confronted with what is about to ruin it all. Although, I doubt James cares about what I want right now. I doubt he will care ever again.

"James?"

He hasn't moved. I don't even see his chest rising and falling. He slowly turns around, cautiously rotating step by step. There is a blue watch in his hand. His eyes are wide and lifeless.

"Where did you get this?" he asks monotonously.

I don't want to lie to him again, but the truth cannot seem to escape my mouth. I only look at him. My silence amplifies his fury.

"*Where did you get this?*" he screams.

PAST

AUGUST 1963

"What took so long, old man?" I say as I run toward the already opened car door. He didn't even want to spend time waiting for me to open it myself. "I thought I was going to have to call again."

He looks around the street frantically before reaching over me and closing the door. "Hey, keep your voice down, please. And you know you can't call me. It's against our rules, remember?" he says.

I roll my eyes. "Yes, yes, Mr. Levins, I remember." He established new "rules" a week ago. I have only complied because it is easier than arguing. I put my seatbelt on and he immediately starts driving.

"I'd appreciate it if you'd be more respectful when speaking to me," he says.

"Hey, you give what you get. It's an equal society now, haven't you heard? The president established the Equal Pay Act two months ago."

"Sure, right, I'm aware, but I do treat you with respect and I expect the same. That's how—how people talk to one another. With mutual respect."

"Aw, I hadn't meant to hurt your feelings, Mr. Levins." I say to him, batting my eyelashes. I am hoping that my charisma will get him to loosen up. He seems very tense. I suppose that it's just one of those days.

He glances at me like he wants to retort but decides against it. Instead, he mumbles something under his breath. I could not decipher any of it save for the word "kid."

"Did you say something?" I ask.

He sighs deeply, then says, "No."

His breath smells vaguely of whisky. "Did you drink?"

He continues to stare at the road. "That's not important."

I do not pry further.

He is never very talkative during these drives. "Could you turn on the radio?" I ask. He turns the frequency to the first station he can find. He seems like he is glad to have a barrier between us and conversing. "Be My Baby" by The Ronettes begins to play. I hum along to the melody.

I like that David is quiet. Some people just never stop talking. Although he speaks very fast, he only talks when necessary. He stutters slightly, too. I wonder if he is like that with other people as well, or if the quavers in his voice are reserved for me only. I prefer the latter. It is one more thing that is ours alone.

I met David several months ago. I had just moved to the city, and I had no idea what I was doing or

where I was going. While I was wandering in the
financial district, he aggressively bumped into me. My
purse fell to the ground, and as I crouched to pick it
up, cursing him under my breath, I heard him scurry
back toward me. "I am so sorry ma'am. I didn't mean
to do that, I'm just in a hurry," he quickly spurted as he
picked my purse up for me. He offered his hand to
help me up and as he finally looked at me, he simply
exhaled, "Wow." I happened to run into him again
later that day. We got to talking and, to make a long
story short, we had sex in the back of his car. After we
were done, he wearily asked me how old I was. I told
him I was eighteen. I was sixteen and a half. Whether
he genuinely believed me or only chose to is not
something I can know for certain.

David is scrawny—which contributes to his slightly
sunken face—and barely taller than I am. Though, to
be fair, I am five-foot ten. Nonetheless, he takes care of
himself. His light-brown hair is always styled in a gelled
comb over, and he is never unshaven. However, none
of this is what first attracted me to David. What really
allured me to him, the forty-five-year-old man who had
shoved into me so hard I nearly fell on my bottom, was
his eyes. David's eyes are a shade of blue so dark you
might confuse them for brown in the wrong lighting.
It is a unique feature, one that captured my interest
instantly.

Nevertheless, David's charm is his defining feature.
Even if he had the most forgettable eyes in the world,
David Levins knows how to make a girl swoon. During

one of our recent dalliances, he followed the curvature of my naked body with his finger and said, "If I could replicate what I am tracing right now on a canvas, it would look like a renaissance painting." It is a large contrast from the boundaries he is suddenly trying to set with me. He only says stuff like that right before or right after sex, though—his lust overpowers his guilt. Maybe today he is just feeling particularly guilty. Maybe his wife cooked him an especially good dinner.

Mom used to tell me, "*Tra moglie e marito non mettere il dito.*" Never interfere between a husband and a wife. She never spoke much Italian apart from the proverbs she thought counted as wisdom. The first time she said that to me was when I first saw her bathing Dad. I must have been five years old. Usually, I would be asleep when she bathed him, but I had had a nightmare that night.

I remember what it was. I was in a long hallway, completely dark apart from a lit candle in the distance. From the light, I could see the color of the walls—a white so void of shadow it looked celestial. Mom was holding the candle. She smiled when she saw me, her teeth the same color as the walls that surrounded us. She began to walk toward me. As she approached, I could see that my eyes had mistaken me earlier. In one hand, she held a slice of vanilla cake with a candle atop it. In the other, she held the hand of Dad, who she was dragging behind her.

"Happy birthday," she said. "Make a wish."

I looked down at Dad who stared blankly ahead. I took in a breath and slowly released it as I blew out the candle. The bright white of the walls disappeared and everything went black.

When I woke, I heard the splashing of water from the bathroom. I stood at the door frame and watched as soap trickled down Dad's limp body. I hadn't showered for two weeks by then. Mom turned around and saw me staring. She looked very angry at me. I wasn't sure what I had done wrong. It would not be the last time I felt like that. It was then that she told me, "*Tra moglie e marito non mettere il dito.* Get back to bed."

She used that saying as an excuse for herself. A reassurance that her negligence toward me was valid so long as her marriage was surviving. That the way I was parented was between her and her husband. That everything was between a man and a woman. I'm sure that if she saw me with David now, she would shun me again. *Tra moglie e marito non mettere il dito.* But what did she know about anything? David might be ashamed of our predicament, but that is a problem he has with himself. I am not an interference. No one is forcing him to call me at night. He is old enough to make his own decisions, and this is what he is choosing. I do not ask questions about why he does it, and I do not judge him for it.

Despite everything, David is not a bad person. He is sensitive and gentle. He sincerely loves his family. He talks about his son quite often, a man I believe is only about three years my senior, James.

David told me about how James has recently moved to Midtown from Brooklyn to pursue photography. I have never seen a father express such open admiration for his son. Many men believe they are too masculine to do so. David isn't like that. He is caring and authentic and regardless of his guilty hedonism, I am grateful for the piece of him I carry.

David drives us all the way from the East of Midtown to River Park in the Bronx in his 1957 Ford Thunderbird, a model I only know because he told me all about it. In his defense, I did ask about it. In my defense, I did not think there was so much to say about cars. How mistaken I was. There is an exhaust, an engine, a motor, a dashboard, and a frame. My, and there are like a million variations. It's never-ending! No woman should ever be cursed with having a man explain to her what in the world "horsepower" is. Whatever happened to an engine, a wheel, and four tires. When did everything get so complicated?

Apart from our first meeting, every one of the interactions between David and I have happened at night. It has never bothered me. We are both there with the same goal and the time of day does not affect the way I feel. I am not a child. I can understand the lengths David goes to hide this infidelity. The only issue this time is that we are in a park far from all the bright buildings. I can't see a thing.

When we arrive, David exits the car and opens the door for me. He does not offer his hand to support me. I look around as he closes the door and turns off the engine. The only potential source of light is from the lanterns placed by a rock, seemingly for public use. David lights one for me and one for himself as we begin to walk. I am very confused about how this is supposed to be enticing.

"David, this does not seem like a great place to perform our usual activities," I say as I swat away the mosquitoes that are beginning to eat me alive.

I wore a pink shift dress for tonight knowing that it is an easily removable article of clothing. My hair is simply brushed back under a headband. The only makeup I have applied is light pink lipstick and mascara. Why make an effort when you know it will get ruined in under an hour?

We approach a small wooden bridge. His pace slows as I try to appreciate the scenery. There is not much to see beyond what the lantern allows me to. I can see the dirt-paved path we walk on, glimpses of trees, flowers, and the swarms of mosquitoes. As we walk on the bridge, I cannot even see the river streaming below me. Objects that are typically ethereal in the daylight are now displayed as black silhouettes. The world has been consumed by shadows.

When we reach the middle of the bridge, David turns to me. "I need to discuss something with you. It's important—rather crucial—to the state of our relationship. You and me…"

You and I, I correct in my head.

"I just—I hope you can understand, I—I know this is not—I have told better news and I—"

"Spit it out, David," I interrupt.

"I don't think we should see each other anymore." He says it so fast it sounds like one word.

"What?"

"My wife. I—I need to be a better husband for her. To put the energy that I put into this philandering into my relationship with her."

"I thought you said that she doesn't sleep with you anymore."

He supports himself on the railing. "She—She doesn't, but that's the problem, you see. It's my responsibility to fix that, to—to get her excited about marriage again. About me again. And I can't do that and still be with you. This has been wrong. I'm—I am a bad person for this. And I'm sorry for dragging you into it, but you're still young and there are men out there who are much better than I am. Right now, I need to make things right with my wife. James moving out is a sign—a sign from God—that now is my opportunity to rekindle my marriage. Fix my mistakes. This—this was a mistake, and it needs to stop."

He looks at me expectantly, waiting for my response. It is a lot of information to absorb, but I am doing so, slowly. David is leaving me to spend more time with a wife that hardly spares him a glance. A wife he has not slept with in years. I have become disposable.

David is not a bad man. I can see that. But he just did a bad thing. I won't be neglected. Not for a woman so dull and prim that she cannot satisfy her own husband. He needed *me*, not her. People need someone who will make them feel loved. He feels nothing with her.

"I don't understand," I say blankly.

His expression turns from placating to impatient. "It's over. I'll drive you back. We—you can—can sleep restfully and forget about all this. I will be in Brooklyn. The only woman I will ever tou—make love to again will be my wife. We are not seeing each other again."

Have you ever been so enraged that you enter a somatic state? Your mind—replaced by your corporeal being. In such cases, there is only animalistic instinct to protect you, doing its best at navigating a consciousness that values sensibility. It is unrealistic to expect an animal to be successful at doing so. An animal does not care to be sensible. It only knows to covet and conquer. So when I push David off the bridge, I do not hesitate.

I hear his yelp, followed by a crack and a subsequent squelch. I don't suppose he had a soft landing.

I walk down the bridge, lantern in hand as I approach the stream. David lies with his skull caved into the shape of the rock he lays on. I walk further toward him. The illumination of the lantern causes a glare from something on his wrist. It's a watch. An expensive limited edition. There is a racing chronograph with attached deep blue leather straps.

David told me that James had gotten him the watch before moving to Manhattan as a thank you for all that he has done for him. There is a tiny engravement of the letters "D.M.L" on the leather. David's initials.

I do not look at his face. I do not allow myself to. My gaze is only directed toward his wrist.

I find myself unclasping the watch gradually, delicately. I do not know what compels me to do so. It is simply an impulse that I cannot defy. I place it in my brasserie, and I return to the car.

I look in the trunk for anything that may give the indication that David was here with another person. There is nothing except for a first aid box and a bottle of whisky.

I open the first aid box, using my dress as protection from my hands. I make gloves for myself with the gauze and begin to think about what I might have touched, any time I may have left fingerprints. I am filled with relief when I realize there have not been many. David had been doing all the work. My hands were in my lap the entire drive, fidgeting with my nails in excitement. Little did I know.

There are only two things that I know I touched for certain. The lantern and David. I do not waste a minute.

First, I walk deep in the forest, shatter the lantern, then bury it. I bury it deep enough so that there is the possibility it would be found but dismissed because it will appear to have simply been abandoned long ago. Then I take a bandage, pour a moderate amount of

whisky on it, and I approach David. This time, I do
not care about his face. I do not care about what I was
planning on doing when we drove here. I do not care
about who he was to me twenty minutes ago. All I care
about is rescuing myself. And if this is what I must do,
then so be it.

I begin to dab the whisky-soaked gauze onto his
chest, alcohol slathering the area where I shoved him
only minutes before. I place the first aid box and the
whisky back in the trunk exactly as I found it. I carry
the alcohol-infused bandage, gauze gloves, and watch
as I begin making my way back to midtown. After I
walk for approximately a mile, I bury the bandage.
Two miles later, I bury the gloves. The watch remains
in my brasserie. By the fourth mile, I consider taking
the subway, but I could not do so even if my life
depended on it—which it terribly may. I cannot pay
the fare. I do not have a single cent on my person, let
alone fifteen. So, I continue to walk.

As I make my way through the Upper East Side, I
wonder what the time is. The sky is still as black as
pitch, but few people still stroll outside. It is strange for
one to be walking through this part of Manhattan this
late at night. I avoid any contact with other people.

The pink dress was a terrible idea, too noticeable,
too memorable. And even worse when you're
surrounded by the posh. But, to my luck, I make it to
midtown with no human interaction apart from an
occasional disdainful glance. I am going to burn this
dress first thing in the morning. There are many more

people here which hopefully means that a woman swaddling to her apartment becomes more forgetful. Who cares about a woman scurrying about when you're in New York City on a Friday night?

When I enter my apartment, the first thing I do is strip off my clothes and prepare to shower. As I remove my dress, I remember the watch that remains huddled in my brassiere. I place it on the side of the bathtub as I shower. I scrub soap on my body three times over and shampoo my hair twice. When I finish, I put the dress in a paper shopping bag. I know an alley I can visit tomorrow, and I have a lighter for my cigarettes laid upon the ashtray on my kitchen counter. I dress myself in a nightgown and place the watch in the bottom drawer of my nightstand, below some magazines. I then climb into bed and place my blanket around my shoulders.

I do not think about why I did what I did. When I close my eyes, I am not haunted by the images that laid before me several hours ago. Like a caterpillar on a leaf, a fish in the sea, or a bird in the sky, I have never felt more at peace.

I hum a lullaby to myself as I drift asleep.

CURRENT

MARCH 1968

"I was in love with David and...he never appreciated it. I was his dirty secret. The girl he ran to so he could escape his life and his marriage. When he said he was going to leave me, I lost control. I just acted. But I didn't feel about him the way I feel about you, James. You were different."

Those last sentences catch his attention. I've said the wrong thing.

"Is this supposed to be helping your point?" he says incredulously.

I cannot take it back now, so I say, "There is no 'point.' I am not trying to defend myself—"

"'Different,'" he interrupts. "I was 'different.' You are just unbelievable. When we were together, hidden behind all your endearment, was the fact that none of this was a new experience for you. This was just another version of something that has already happened...Oh God, the amount of things I must have done that reminded you of him." His hand lingers over his heart. "All that I have told you about him. All that I have told you about how much it devastated me.

When he died, I couldn't eat, I couldn't sleep. I couldn't bring myself to talk to my family. I was haunted by my memories with him. I lost the person who was the foundation for everything about me. And two years later…I fell in love with the person who took him from me? The woman who was his mistress? I made love to you. I wanted to marry you. I thought that my life would begin and end with you. And you *let me.*"

I do not say anything.

He looks into my eyes. "Know that there will never exist a word that expresses the extent in which I *despise* you. I wish my father did so much worse to you. I wish he had thought first to be the one to—" He swallows his words. "I want to say that no man will ever love you again, but you are conniving and manipulative. I know that I won't be the last. You will bed men who will become infatuated with your beauty. They will obsess over the model you portray. They will fall for your act, but they will never fall for you."

He begins to laugh to himself, as if his bafflement is becoming humorous, now. "It's unsurprising that you're not religious. It all pieces together now. You're too scared of what's waiting for you when you die. After everything, all you will ever be is flesh in dirt. The only thing willing to touch you will be the maggots feasting on your rotten soul." He spits on the floor in front of me.

I was overgenerous when describing his reaction earlier. He was just too shocked to say how he really felt. Now that he has come back to reality, he is merciless with his words. I know what I did was wrong, but this behavior is demeaning. I have let him express his anger—I no longer have to tolerate being degraded.

"How dare you?" I say.

This takes him by surprise. "How dare *I?*" He points a finger at me. "Do you understand what you did? Am I giving you too much credit? Are you so absent-minded that you just don't understand the severity of it? Do you not understand just how evil you are? Did you not even think to break up with me when you found out who—"

He pauses. There is clearly more he wants to say. He would do this for the next three days if I just stood here and let him. Instead, he pauses and looks at me. His bloodshot eyes are watering—I don't think he has blinked in the last ten minutes— and it is a scary look. This is the man who, not even twenty-four hours ago, I was beginning to envision the rest of my life with. I believed that if I just distanced him from his mother, our love would prevail. I am all too familiar with how quick life can change in a moment. This is like meeting an old friend. As his eyebrows furrow, I recognize that he has come to a revelation. He looks like he is battling even saying it. I know the feeling.

"Did you orchestrate all this—our relationship? Am I my own father's fucking replacement?"

This is not getting any easier.

PAST

After David died, I felt myself gravitate toward his ghost. My body searched for his warmth and was greeted by a breeze. I hadn't realized that through all the clandestine rendezvous, I had begun to crave him. I would wait for his calls and seek out his gazes, however ephemeral they may have been. The longer I went without them, the more my soul ached. I could not withstand the feeling of loss. I needed a man like David to love me and only me. But I would not let myself become trapped as a wife. I wanted freedom and love simultaneously. If it were not for Elizabeth, I would have achieved it with David.

Elizabeth, Elizabeth, Elizabeth. She had destroyed everything. But it wasn't over for me. I wanted to prove that I could defeat her, and I yearned for David's touch again, so I settled for the second-best thing. A year after David died, I began to search for James Levins.

It is very difficult to learn things about someone you have never met, but I did have something. I knew that James was a photographer, that he was attending Columbia University, and that he lived in Manhattan.

I took the bus to fourteenth avenue, then I took the IRT subway up Broadway to get to the school. I visited the admissions office inquiring about their arts program. I asked about their current attendees, as well. The receptionist there did not mention James's name, but I wrote down the names of the others and took the subway back home. I called each of them, introducing myself with a different name each time. "Hello, my name is Anna Smith," I said first. For the next call, "Hi, I am Barbara Gould." I continued forward with, "Hello, Judy Greene calling." But for each of the calls, I would present the same circumstance, "I am an old friend of James Levins from high school and I heard that you went to college with him, is there any way you can tell me where he works now? I would love to catch up."

The first three people said that they did not personally know James, so I said my thanks then hung up.

After the fourth attempt I—disguised as Margaret Jones—called someone, a man named Robert Andrews.

"James? Of course! He's a great guy, yeah. He and I are buddies, not super close. He can be a little quiet sometimes. A strange guy at times but charismatic too, yeah. How was he in high school?"

"Oh, quite the same. I am sure he has changed though. It's been a while since I've spoken to him."

"Aw, why? Was it the distance? I know how it is. High school ends, people go off to college, lose touch.

It's unfortunate, yeah. I had so many friends in high school and lost, like, half of them to distance alone. It's hard, y'know? How am I 'sposed to keep in touch if I'm in New York and you're in Pennsylvania. Lost some good people. Even a girl, yeah," he said with a sigh.

I was rather agitated that the one person with information on James was so garrulous. "Right, yes, it happens, I know, a very tragic thing. But—" I attempt, but he interrupts.

"Yeah, Jane was my soulmate, y'know? I was on the football team 'cause I like football, but I *love* art. I really dig it, y'know? Painting—my true passion, yeah. Jane always got that. She really got me. 'Lots of girls are just phonies. They want you because you play football, but they don't dig your true self, y'know? Not Jane, though. I miss her a lot, I really do. I wonder what she's doing right now."

I understood that if I did not redirect this conversation, it wouldn't end until I was thirty. "Yes, yes. So, I've been thinking about James, and now I want to revitalize our friendship. Ensure that distance does not ruin anything. Would you happen to know where he works by chance? I'd love to visit him and catch up."

Robert giggled on the other line. "Oh, did you two have some sort of romance?"

I tried to interrupt, but he continued. "Don't worry, don't worry. I understand. And with what I just told you about Jane and I...It must've been hard to hear about that, must've scared 'ya. But don't worry, it would be my pleasure to help rekindle some puppy love. Maybe you guys can have what I lost with Jane..." I think I heard him sniffle. "But, hey, Ms. Jones, if it's in my hands, I am going to make sure you two find each other again. I know how it feels to love someone and not want 'em to go, yet they do, yeah."

I bit my tongue to try and restrain myself from retorting. Robert Andrews was unendurable.

Finally, he provided me with what I wanted to know. "Jamie told me that he works in the Chock Full o' Nuts on 34th street. You want me to tell him you called? I'm sure he'll appreciate it."

I told him it wasn't necessary, then I thanked him for being so helpful and happily hung up the phone.

I let enough time pass for James to forget about Margaret Jones, just in case Robert had told him about the call. A very conceivable possibility, honestly, I doubt that he didn't. I also wanted to ensure that James would not still be in mourning. I knew that he and his father were close.

In March, I began to visit Chock Full o' Nuts regularly. There were many people at the coffee shop, which meant more waiters and a reduced chance that James would be the one serving me. I feared that I would not be able to recognize him, that perhaps he looked entirely like his mother. But as my eyes searched the room, I was quickly able to identify James Levins.

He was tall and lean like his father, but more muscular. He was blonde, which I was not expecting, but the most distinguishing characteristic he acquired were his eyes. Those deep blue eyes that I could never resist on David were passed on to his son. I would stay in the area for hours, learning James's schedule. I considered following him after his shifts, but I abstained. I wanted him to personally show me the places he visited for leisure, so I settled for visiting his work. Earl, the owner, guilelessly regarded me as a revisiting customer. He truly is a wonderful man. I would talk to him any time I saw him.

Once I learned James's schedule, I only came during the hours he worked. Which, painfully, were when the store was busiest. The only shift where the crowds were reasonable was the shift that lasted from six o'clock to noon. Eventually, in April of 1965, during one of those morning shifts, James Levins asked me for my order.

I suppose what made James believe our love was so exceptional was because it was serendipitous. Gradually, I am deteriorating James's perception of the last three years. But I can't change it now. And there is no use in lying to James anymore.

———————————————

"Yes, I... searched for you," I say.

Although James has been devastated throughout this entire conversation, his expression turns into one so grim that I know that I have just ruined his life.

CURRENT

MARCH 1968

"My father..." His father? His father was a participant in our relationship. James believes that David was a saint, which leaves me playing the role of the devil. Just because I did something bad does not mean that David didn't. Bad choices lead to bad circumstances.

"James, your father wasn't perfect. He was the one calling me. You are treating me like I did what I did sadistically. I did love David, but I felt betrayed. I thought my life was over without him. I was lost and scared. And you are treating me like—like some callous criminal. Like you never loved me and I never loved you. I know what I did was wrong and I have apologized for it."

"Do you regret it?"

My words mean nothing to him.

"What?" I ask.

"If you could go back and never meet him, never meet me, would you?"

Meeting David allowed me to meet James. I do not know where I would have been without him. I do not think I would ever want to know.

"No, I wouldn't."

I know that my answer is not what James wants to hear, but he deserves to know the truth.

James nods to himself. Then, he takes a glass vase—the one that once housed the flowers that he gave me before he asked to marry me—and throws it at my head.

I leap back to avoid it which results in me tripping over a box on the floor. Before I get the chance to properly react, James swiftly walks up to me, crouches, takes a piece of broken glass, and points it at my neck.

My body loses all its mobility. "James, you're acting like a lunatic."

"Are you hearing yourself?" he says bitterly.

There is no use in explaining myself anymore. All I can do is watch as he drives himself mad, hating me.

James continues, "You're a poison. You will never understand the magnitude of what you did. You will never understand the treachery of it. I devoted myself to you as you vowed to destroy everything I love...You murdered my father...and you're still alive. Why are *you* still alive? How is that fair?"

I look down at the sharp piece of glass still inches away from my throat, his hand hovers beside my shoulder. His grip is so firm that his palm begins to bleed, painting the glass red.

"You can make your peace with this however you choose, James. I can't take that away from you," I say.

James stares at me. Never did I think that my favorite thing about James Levins would become so harrowing so quickly. Even still, I look into his eyes and despite all of it, I love him. I have learned to love James for all that he is. If only he did the same for me.

His hand trembles as droplets of his blood fall graciously on my shoulder. He's scared. My life, a compilation of all my memories, something only accessible to me, purged from existence within a hand's movement.

Our breathing begins to sync—the closest to unison we will ever get to each other again. James raises the glass shard, and I force my eyes shut, preparing for the excruciating pain that awaits me. But I don't feel anything. I open my eyes to see the glass dropping to the floor. It lands with a *clank.*

James begins to take steps backward, away from me. His eyes move rapidly between me and the glass shard he had just directed toward my neck. His facial expression remains neutral, but I know him better than to fall for the confident front he is putting on. I know that he is ashamed of himself, horrified that he let himself get as far as he did. He glances down at his bleeding hand. The drops of blood stain the rug below him.

I hear police sirens approaching. A neighbor must have heard the yelling, the glass shattering, and called them.

Unless James decides to tell his mother the truth—which I don't think he will—no one, apart from him, will know anything. This was just a fight between lovers. "We were having an argument and the vase fell,"

I'll tell the police. "The noise was just from James profusely apologizing and insisting that he buy me a new one. Isn't he a sweetheart?"

James will not be here by the time they arrive. He is already grabbing his car keys and walking toward the door. He will leave this apartment and then he will leave New York. There is not a single doubt in my mind about it. The man who fought to marry me will spend the rest of his life trying to avoid me.

Though, I do not want it to end quite yet. I need to remind him that he has not won. He will never win. Whether it is in person or in a magazine, in the afterlife or in his nightmares, this is not the last time we will be meeting.

It is the people we cannot forgive that we never forget, and James will never forgive me.

"See you soon, dear," I choke out. His movement slows. There is a moment where I think he might stop, might retort, but James Levins walks out the door without sparing me a second glance.

The End.

ACKNOWLEDGEMENTS

I have many people to thank for helping and supporting me during the process of writing *Mr. Levins and Me*. To begin, I want to thank my family: Ben, Shir, Ema, and Aba. Thank you all for reading this and being so supportive. I was nervous about writing this book, and you all made me feel like this could be something beyond words on a document. Every time I doubt myself, you are the ones I go to for the reassurance that I am capable. I hold immense value to your opinions. Your faith in me has helped me throughout my whole life and it will continue to do so as I grow up. You are the most important people in my life—I cannot thank you enough for everything you all do for me.

I especially want to thank my sister, Shir. Shir, although I can be an irritable little sister, I want you to know how much I appreciate you. You are my best friend, and I am so thankful that you were the one who illustrated this cover. I could not have asked for someone better to do it. I love that this feels like something I can share with you. I am proud to be your sister, and I thank you wholeheartedly.

Next, I want to thank Noga Shachak. Noga, you not only took the time to edit this novella word for word, but you also supplied me with brilliant advice on how to improve it. Your patience, your kindness, and your goodwill have shone throughout this process. This book would not have been complete without you, and I am so grateful to you for it. Thank you tremendously.

I also want to thank the people who read this while I was still writing it, Sierra and Ricky. It's one thing to hear support from family but another to hear it from friends. You both made *Mr. Levins and Me* feel authentic. You gave me the opportunity to show my work to an audience. More than that, you uplifted me when I was nervous about my writing. I loved being able to laugh at your reactions as you progressed through the book. Thank you both for believing in me; I appreciate it more than you know.

Lastly, I want to thank my grade 12 English teacher, Mr. Mobedi. In the final days of the semester, you told me, "Lior, you know, if you don't already, you should really write stories. You've got something." It was fleeting to you, but it meant the world to me. I would not have even thought of doing that without you. You ignited my motivation to start this book. Your words helped me sit down and write a story. Thank you.